The Crooked House

Brandon Fleming

The Crooked House

The present edition is a reproduction of previous publication of this classic work. Minor typographical errors may have been corrected without note, however, for an authentic reading experience the spelling, punctuation, and capitalization have been retained from the original text.

ISBN: 978-1-64439-173-0

CONTENTS

THE CROOKED HOUSE

Chapter I

A Strange Riddle

"Monsieur Tranter! A moment!"

The Right-Honorable John Tranter swung round, latch-key in hand. Behind him, an enormous figure emerged, with surprisingly agile and noiseless steps, from the shadow of the adjoining house—a figure almost grotesque and monstrous in the dim light of the street lamp. The very hugeness of the apparition was so disconcerting that John Tranter drew back with a startled exclamation.

"Good Lord! Monsieur Dupont? You in London?"

Monsieur Dupont described circles with his country's largest silk hat.

"I in London! An event, my friend, in the history of your city!"

He laughed softly, and replaced the hat on his head. They shook hands warmly.

"This is a delightful surprise," Tranter said, turning back to the door. "Come in."

"It is late," Monsieur Dupont apologized—"but I entreat a moment. It is three hours only since I arrived, and I have passed one of them on your doorstep."

"An hour?" Tranter exclaimed. "But surely——"

Monsieur Dupont squeezed himself into the narrow hall with difficulty.

"I possess the gift of patience," he claimed modestly. "In London it is of great value."

In the small library he looked about him with surprise. The plain, almost scanty furniture of Tranter's house evidently did not accord with his expectations of the residence of an English Privy Councillor. Monsieur Dupont sat down on a well-worn leather couch, and stared, somewhat blankly, at the rows of dull, monotonous bindings in the simple mahogany bookcases.

He placed the drink Tranter mixed for him on a small table by his side, accepted a cigar, and puffed at it serenely. And in that position, Monsieur Victorien Dupont presented a pleasing picture of elephantine geniality. He was so large that his presence seemed to fill half the room. His great face was one tremendous smile. His eyes, though capable of a disconcertingly direct gaze, were clear and even childlike. His English was perfect, his evening-dress faultless, and, though obviously a bon-viveur, he was also unmistakably a man with a purpose.

"And what has brought you to London?" Tranter asked, sitting opposite to him.

"My friend," said Monsieur Dupont, "I am here with a remarkable object. I have come to use the eyes the good God has given me. And to do so I beg the assistance of the great position the good God has given you."

"I hope," Tranter returned, "that what you require will enable me to make some sort of return to the man who saved my life."

Monsieur Dupont waved his hands in a gigantic gesture.

"To restore to the world one of its great men—it was a privilege for which I, myself, should pay! The service I ask of you is small."

"You have but to name it," said the Privy Councillor.

Suddenly there was no smile on Monsieur Dupont's face. Without the smile it was a very much less pleasant face.

"Two years ago, in my own country," his voice acquired a new snap, "some one asked me a riddle."

"A riddle?" Tranter echoed, surprised at the change.

"A very strange riddle. Unfortunately, I cannot tell you what it was. I cannot tell any one what it was. I undertook to find the answer. From France the riddle took me far away to another country—and there, after a year's work, I found half the answer. The other half is in London. And I am in London to find it."

"This is interesting," said Tranter, smiling slightly at the huge Frenchman's intense seriousness.

"You, my friend, can help me."

"I am at your service," the other promised.

Monsieur Dupont half-emptied his glass, and the smile began to reappear on his face in gradual creases. In a moment the shadow had vanished. He laughed like a jolly giant.

"Ah, forgive me! I had almost committed the crime to be serious. It is a fault that is easy in your London."

"What do you want me to do for you?" Tranter asked.

"I want," said Monsieur Dupont, "to be taken with you, as your friend from Paris, to one or two society functions—where I may be likely to meet ... what I seek."

Tranter was somewhat taken aback.

"Unconsciously," he returned—"though of course, I will make it my business to fulfill your wishes—you have really asked me a difficult thing. No man goes less into society than I do. Most people have given up inviting me."

"Forgive me," said Monsieur Dupont again. "I had imagined I should be asking a thing the most simple."

"So you are," Tranter assured him. "The fault is with me. Where women are concerned I am utterly hopeless. I fly from a pretty woman as you might fly from a crocodile."

"An ugly woman," said Monsieur Dupont, "is the real friend of man—if he would but know it."

"The dull family dinners of dull family people are the only 'functions' I ever attend. However, let me see what can be done for you." Tranter rose, and with an amused expression began to sort out a small pile of cards on the mantel-piece.

Monsieur Dupont smiled on. He emptied his glass, and inhaled the smoke of his excellent cigar with all the enjoyment of a satisfied connoisseur. His glance played from one article of furniture to another, from the floor to the ceiling, from bookcase to bookcase, from picture to picture. The very plainness of the room seemed to fascinate him. His gaze sought out the ugliest picture, and became fixed on it. Tranter turned over all the cards, and shrugged his shoulders helplessly.

"In a couple of days I shall be able to fix you up a dozen times over," he said. "But I am afraid I have scarcely anything to offer you for to-morrow night. Why didn't you drop me a line in advance?"

"Let us dispense with to-morrow night, then," said Monsieur Dupont.

Tranter ran through the cards again.

"There is a dinner at Lord Crumbleton's—which I have too much regard for you to suggest. The Countess is a most estimable lady, who has spent the last fifteen years in vain attempts to become unfaithful to her husband, and now reads the Apocrypha all day for stimulation. You could dine with a high-church clergyman who absolves sins, or an actor-manager who commits them. But stay——" he paused quickly. "I forgot. There is something else." He sorted out a card. "Here is a possibility of amusement that had escaped me."

"Ah!" said Monsieur Dupont.

"George Copplestone has favored me wit an invitation to a select gathering at his house at Richmond, which would be very much more likely to provide answers to riddles. I never accept Copplestone's invitations on principle—although he goes on sending them. But, if you like, I will break my rule, and take you. It is sure to be entertaining, if nothing more."

Monsieur Dupont bowed his gratitude. Tranter replaced the cards, and returned to his seat.

"Copplestone is a remarkable individual, who has learnt what a multitude of sins even a slight financial connection with the Theater will cover. He puts various sums of money into the front of the house to gain unquestioned admission to the back. He has an extraordinary taste for fantasy, and is always startling his friends with some new eccentricity. He is not generally considered to be a desirable acquaintance—and certainly no man in London has less regard for the conventions."

"To confine myself to desirable acquaintances," said Monsieur Dupont, "would be my last wish."

"Then we will go to Richmond to-morrow night. He lives in a very strange house, in a stranger garden—the sort of place that no ordinary normal person could possibly live in. And I warn you that you will find nothing ordinary or normal in it. If you are interested in some of the unaccountable vagaries of human nature, you will enjoy yourself."

"The unaccountable vagaries of human nature," said Monsieur Dupont, "are the foundation of my riddle."

"Then," Tranter returned, "I could give you no better chance to solve it. In addition, you will probably make the acquaintance of a certain pretty society widow, who wants to marry him because of his vices, and one or two other well-known people who owe him money and can't afford to refuse to dine with him. Also, as the invitation is an unusually pressing one, we can rely on the introduction of some unexpected freaks for our entertainment."

"It is arranged," Monsieur Dupont declared, "I go with you to Richmond."

"Very well," Tranter agreed. "Call for me here at eight o'clock, and we will go. Help yourself to another drink."

Monsieur Dupont helped himself to another drink.

Chapter II

The Crooked House

It was no unusual thing for George Copplestone to spring surprises on his guests. He had a twisted sense of the dramatic, and twisted things were expected from him. On some occasions he perpetrated the wildest and most extravagant eccentricities, without the slightest regard for the moral or artistic sensibilities of those on whom he imposed them—on others he contented himself with less harrowing minor freaks—but the object of thoroughly upsetting and confounding the mental balances of his victims was invariably achieved. He delighted, and displayed remarkable ingenuity, in providing orgies of the abnormal. He reveled in producing an atmosphere of brain-storm, and in dealing sledge-hammer blows at the intellects of his better balanced acquaintances. Often he was in uncontrollable spirits—on fire with mental and physical exuberance—sometimes he was morose and silent, and apparently weak. Frequently he disappeared for considerable periods, and his house appeared to be closed. But none saw his coming or going.

Strange rumors circulated about him from time to time. Certain social circles, to which his wealth and position entitled him to the entrée, were closed to him. Over and above his wild extravagancies, he was credited with vices that remained unnamed. It was said that things took place in his house that sealed the lips of men and women. When his name was mentioned in the clubs, some men shrugged their shoulders. When it was spoken in the drawing-rooms, some women remained silent. There had been an attempt to stab him, and twice he had been shot at. After the second attempt, a woman had been heard to say bitterly that he must bear a charmed life. He continued to pursue his strange ways with supreme indifference to the opinions of his fellow-creatures.

The house he lived in was the only sort of house he could have lived in. From the foundations to the topmost brick it was a mass of bewildering crookedness. Nothing was straight. Not a single passage led where it would have been expected to lead—not a staircase fulfilled normal anticipations. Scarcely two windows in the whole building were the same size—scarcely two rooms were the same shape—and not even two contortions corresponded. There must have been a mile of unnecessary corridors, dozens of incomprehensible corners and turnings, and at least a score of unwanted entrances and exits. If the aim and object of the architect, whoever he was, had been to reduce the unfortunate occupants of his handiwork to a condition of hopeless mental entanglement, he could not have created a more effective instrument for the purpose. George Copplestone found it a residence after his own heart, and delighted in the means it provided for gratifying his feverish inspirations.

The room into which John Tranter and Monsieur Victorien Dupont were ushered at eight-thirty on the following night presented an extraordinary spectacle of lavish and indiscriminate decoration, arriving at a general suggestion of something between a Royal visit and preparations for a wildly enthusiastic Christmas. Flags and festoons, flowers, real and imitation, fairy-candles and colored lamps, burning with strange heavy scents, quaint fantastic shapes of paper, startlingly illuminated—all massed into an indescribable disorder of light and color. Five amazed people were awaiting further developments.

Mrs. Astley-Rolfe was a charming widow of twenty-seven, who had successfully gambled on her late husband's probable lease of life, and was now in the throes of a wild attachment to George Copplestone, to which he had shown himself by no means averse. She was somewhat languid from an excess of luxury, unable to brook opposition even to a whim, and as yet undefeated in the attainment of her desires, which were not, perhaps, always to the credit of her sex. She had an insufficient income, and a weakness for inscribing her signature on stamped slips of paper, several of which, it was rumored, were in Copplestone's possession. Her house in Grosvenor Gardens was an artistic paradise, and was frequently visited by gentlemen from Jermyn Street, who seemed fond of assuring themselves that its treasures remained intact.

A West-End clergyman, of Evangelical appearance, who translated French farces under a nom-de-plume, was advocating, in confidence, the abolition of the Censor to a well-known theatrical manager, whose assets were all in the name of his wife. A bejeweled Russian danseuse, who spoke broken English with a Highland accent, extolled the attractions of theatrical investment to a Hebrew financier, who was feasting his eyes on the curves of her figure, and hoping that she was sufficiently hard-up. The entrance of Tranter and his huge companion created general surprise. Mrs. Astley-Rolfe held up her hands prettily.

"You?" she exclaimed, to Tranter. "You—of all people—condescending to visit our plane? The mystery is explained at once. The decorations are for you—the Pillar of the State!"

"Indeed they are not," he assured her. He stood aside. "Permit me to introduce my friend, Monsieur Dupont."

"This is delightful!" she smiled.

Monsieur Dupont bent over her hand.

"Madame," he declared, "I change completely my opinion of London."

"Where is Copplestone?" Tranter inquired, gazing with amazement round the festooned room.

A frown passed over Mrs. Astley-Rolfe's face.

"He has not yet appeared. He sent in a message asking us to wait for him here. He is up to some freak obviously."

"It is certainly a strange medley of color," Tranter admitted. "Fortunately, I am not particularly susceptible—but to an artistic temperament I can understand that the effect would be acute. What extraordinary event can such a blaze be intended to celebrate?"

"I don't know," she returned, a little shortly. "He has told us nothing."

Her eyes strayed anxiously to the door. The movements of her hands were nervous.

"I wish he would come," she muttered—and stood away from them.

Tranter drew his companion across the room.

"Well?" he asked, smiling. "How do you like this somewhat showy welcome?"

"My friend," said Monsieur Dupont slowly—"into what manner of house have you brought me?"

"Copplestone is a curious fellow," Tranter replied. "I warned you to be prepared for something unusual."

"It is a crooked house," said Monsieur Dupont. "It stands on a crooked road, and there are crooked paths all round it. And everything is crooked inside it."

"These decorations are crooked enough, at any rate," Tranter laughed.

"These decorations," said Monsieur Dupont, "are not only crooked—they are bad. Very bad."

He lowered his voice. There was a gleam of excitement in his eyes.

"Don't you see," he whispered, "that decorations can be good or bad, just as men and women can be good or bad? These decorations are bad. They are a mockery of all decorations—a travesty the most heartless of the motives for which good and pure people decorate. There is nothing honest or straightforward about them. They are a mean confusion of all the symbols of joy. They are put up for some cruel and detestable purpose——"

7

The door flew open with a snap, and a young man of dishevelled appearance burst into the room. His eyes were wild, and his face was working with the intensity of his passion.

"Christine," he panted. "Christine...."

He stopped, and gazed round in a dazed fashion, clenching and unclenching his hands.

Mrs. Astley-Rolfe sprang forward with a suppressed cry, and confronted him tensely.

"Well?" she cried sharply—"what about Christine?"

He did not seem to be aware of her. He was staring at the flags, the lights, the flowers, and the colored paper.

"It is true then," he muttered. "These things...."

The woman was as white as death. Her hands were locked together. She swayed.

"What is true?" she gasped.

The young man took no notice of her. Copplestone's elderly manservant appeared in the doorway, and approached him.

"Mr. Copplestone declines to see you, sir—and requests that you will leave his house. I have orders, otherwise, to send for the police."

The young man drew himself up. He was suddenly quite composed and dignified. The passion died out of his face, leaving an expression almost of contentment in its place.

"I wish it to be understood," he said, addressing himself to the room generally with perfect evenness, "that, rather than allow Christine Manderson to become engaged to George Copplestone, I will tear her to pieces with my own hands, and utterly destroy her." And he turned, and walked quietly out of the room.

In the silence that followed all eyes were fixed on the white, rigid woman. Her face was drawn and haggard. She seemed to have grown old and weak. Her whole frame appeared to have shrunk under an overwhelming blow. For some moments she stood motionless. Then, with a supreme effort of self-control, she turned, and faced them steadily.

"I think," she said calmly, "that if Miss Manderson is in the house she should be warned."

"Fellow was mad," said the theatrical manager.

"Tout-a-fait daft," agreed the Russian danseuse.

"It would have been safer," Tranter remarked, "if he had been given in charge."

There was something very like contempt in Mrs. Astley-Rolfe's glance.

"Do you know," she said quietly, "that that young man is a millionaire who lives on a pound a week, and spends the remaining

8

nine hundred and ninety-nine pounds a week on saving lives and souls in places in London that people like us try to avoid even hearing about? If it is madness to devote your life and money to lifting some of the world's shadows—then he is very mad."

"Mosth creditable," said the Hebrew financier.

She turned her back on them, and stood apart.

Monsieur Dupont laid a hand on Tranter's arm.

"My friend," he said—and there was the faintest tremor in his voice, "I ask you again—into what manner of house have you brought me?"

"I am beginning to wish that I had not brought you," Tranter returned. "I don't like the atmosphere."

"That," said Monsieur Dupont, drawing him aside, "is where we differ. To me the atmosphere is extremely interesting. If I were a sportsman, I would make you a bet that this will be an eventful evening."

"I feel strongly," said Tranter seriously, "that we should be wise to leave. We don't want to be mixed up in an affair with a madman."

Monsieur Dupont shook his head.

"The millionaire was not mad, my friend. He may have been mad yesterday. He may be mad to-morrow. But he is very sane to-night."

"I don't like it," Tranter maintained. "I would much rather go. Events under this roof have a trick of being a little too dramatic."

Laughter from the clergyman, the financier, and the danseuse, greeted the conclusion of a story with which the theatrical manager had attempted to relieve the strain. Monsieur Dupont drew Tranter still further back.

"This Mademoiselle Manderson—do you know her?"

"No," Tranter replied. "I've never heard of her. I suppose she is some new friend of Copplestone's. If she is really engaged to him, I don't think she is altogether to be envied."

Monsieur Dupont's glance found Mrs. Astley-Rolfe.

"No," he remarked softly—"I do not think she is."

Two heavy curtains at the extreme end of the room were drawn apart, and the figure of a man appeared between them—a tall, thick-set man, in full evening-dress, with a large white flower in his button-hole. For a moment he stood still, looking intently down the room.

"Copplestone," Tranter whispered to his companion.

"Mon Dieu," muttered Monsieur Dupont.

It was the face of a fanatic—wonderful, fascinating, cruel—a fanatic who neither feared God nor regarded man—an infinite egotist. The fires of a great distorted soul smoldered in his eyes. The broad, lofty forehead proclaimed a mind that might have placed him among the rulers of men—but instead he was little above the level of a clown. The destinies of a nation might have rested in the hands that he turned only to selfish fantasy. The whole appearance of him, arresting and almost awe-inspiring as it undoubtedly was, had in it the repulsiveness of the unnatural—and, with that, all the tragedy of pitiful waste.

To-night, he confronted his guests in an attitude, and with an air, of triumph. But as Mrs. Astley-Rolfe turned quickly to him with something of a challenge in her bearing, a faint mocking smile appeared and lingered for a moment on his face. Then he moved aside, his hand on the curtains.

"Ladies and gentlemen," he said deliberately, "permit me to present you to my fiancée—Miss Christine Manderson."

He drew the curtains apart.

"Mon Dieu," said Monsieur Dupont again.

A half-strangled sob came from the lips of Mrs. Astley-Rolfe. Tranter uttered an exclamation. The danseuse, the clergyman, and the theatrical manager burst into vigorous applause.

Framed in the darkness behind him was the white form of a woman, of transcendent loveliness. In the soft light it seemed almost a celestial figure. She smiled with entrancing sweetness, and held out her hands.

But as her gaze swept over the occupants of the room, the smile vanished. Her eyes became fixed and staring; her face set. She uttered a sharp cry—and fell forward in a dead faint.

Chapter III

The Endless Garden

Confusion followed. Copplestone knelt beside her, calling her by name in a strange excess of fear. The theatrical manager tore a flask from his pocket, and administered its contents freely. The spirit revived her. She opened her eyes. They lifted her gently, and laid her on a couch.

"It was that madman rushing in unnerved her," Copplestone cried fiercely. "Wish I'd called in the police. Curse him!"

Her hand closed on his. "No, no," she whispered. "He must not be touched. He didn't mean it."

"Mean it be damned!" said Copplestone savagely. "If I see any more of him, he'll find himself in jail in less time than it takes to say it."

The manager proffered further stimulant. The color began to return to her face, but her eyes were wide and strained. Copplestone watched her closely.

"Look here," said the manager, re-corking his empty flask, "she'd better rest. Let's all clear off, and go on with this another night."

"Thertainly," agreed the financier.

But Christine Manderson rose, and leant on Copplestone's arm. Her self-control was exerted to the utmost, but she trembled.

"Forgive me," she said softly. "I am all right now. Please don't go."

"Good!" Copplestone exclaimed, recovering his equanimity. "It would be a pity to break up. We'll have a jolly night." He laughed loudly. "Tranter, of all people!" he cried boisterously. "And——" he looked towards Monsieur Dupont.

"I was sure you wouldn't mind my bringing a friend with me," Tranter said. "Monsieur Dupont has just arrived from Paris."

"Delighted," said Copplestone, shaking hands with great heartiness. "Forgive this unhappy beginning. We'll make up for it now. Come along to dinner. It's all ready."

In the dining-room they sat down to a table that glittered and gleamed with a hundred lights, concealed under strands of white crystallized leaves, springing from a frosted tree. Such a table might have been set in Fairyland, for the betrothal feast of Oberon.

"Glad we didn't miss this," said the theatrical manager.

He regaled the company with a selection of his less offensive stories, and found ready applause. The gayety was loud and forced.

11

Every one attempted to keep it at fever-heat. Jest followed jest with increasing rapidity. Laughter rang out on the smallest provocation. It was a competition in hilarity. And the gayest of all were Christine Manderson, and Mrs. Astley-Rolfe.

The night was hot and sultry. The distant roll of thunder added to the tenseness of the atmosphere. And hearing it, Christine Manderson shuddered.

"Storms are unlucky to me," she said, listening until the sullen roll died away. "Why should we have one to-night—of all nights?"

The clergyman adroitly twisted the subject of lightning into a compliment. As the dinner drew to a somewhat loud conclusion, Copplestone's face grew flushed, and his hands unsteady. The manager's voice and stories thickened, and the thoughts of the Russian danseuse became fixed on Aberdeen. Tranter and Monsieur Dupont were abstemious guests. But the Frenchman seemed to be enjoying himself immensely.

They rose from the fairy table, and strolled out through the open windows into the garden. The air had grown hotter and more oppressive, the thunder louder. Frequent flashes lit up the darkness.

The glowing tips of cigars and cigarettes disappeared in various directions across the lawns.

Monsieur Dupont discovered, to his cost, the truth of his remark that the house was surrounded by crooked paths. The grounds were a veritable maze. He had purposely slipped away alone, and in five minutes was involved in a network of twisting, thickly-hedged paths, all of which seemed only to lead still further into the darkness.

He stopped, and listened. He could hear no voices. Not a sound, except the gathering thunder, disturbed the silence. He was completely cut off. Even the lights of the house were hidden from him. He had turned about so many times that he did not even know in which direction it lay. Coupled with the effect of what had happened in the house, the influence of this tortuous garden was sinister and unnerving. In the lightning flashes, now more vivid and frequent, he tried in vain to determine his position. He wandered about, trying path after path, doubling back on his own tracks—only to find himself more and more helplessly lost.

"Nom de Dieu," said Monsieur Dupont, in despair.

He halted suddenly, standing as still as a figure of stone. On his right the hedge was thick and high. He could see nothing. But the whisper of a voice had reached him.

The path took a sharp turn. He stepped noiselessly on to the grass border, and crept round, with wonderful agility for a man of his size. The foliage gradually thinned, and kneeling down he was able to listen and peer through until the next flash should reveal what lay beyond.

The whisper thrilled with indescribable passion.

"I love you. You are my body, my soul, my god, my all. I love you—I love you—I love you."

It was the voice of Christine Manderson.

Not a tremor escaped the listener. Parting the leaves with a hand as steady as the ground itself, he waited for the light.

"I have no world but you—no thought but you. I want nothing but you ... you ... you." A sob broke her voice.

"Go," the answer was almost inaudible in its tenseness. "Go—and forget. I have nothing for you."

The lightning came. In a small open space on the other side of the hedge it illuminated the wild tortured face of Christine Manderson. And standing before her, gripping both her hands and holding her away from him—John Tranter.

She struggled to bring herself closer to him.

"I thought you were dead," she gasped.

"I am dead," he answered. "I am dead to you. Let me go."

The listener could almost hear the effort of her breathing.

"I waited for you," she panted. "I was broken. I had to seem happy—but my heart was a tomb. You were all my life—all my hope. I know I wasn't what I might have been. I was what people call an adventuress. But my love for you was the one great, true thing of my life. Oh, why did you leave me?"

"For your own sake," he said slowly. "I am no mate for such a woman as you."

"My own sake?" she repeated. "My own sake—to take from me the only thing I had—my only chance?—to throw my life into the shadows? My own sake ... to have made me what I am?"

"I would have spared you this meeting," he returned, "if I had known. But the name Christine Manderson was strange to me. I had never heard it before."

"I changed my name," she said sadly. "I couldn't bear that any one should use the name that you had used. I called myself Christine Manderson, and went on the stage in New York. Oh, it was dreadful. All those long years since you left me I have lived under a mask—as you have seen me to-night. You thought I was smiling—but I didn't smile. You thought I was laughing—but I didn't laugh. It was all ... only disguised tears ... to hide myself."

"Go," his voice was torn. "For God's sake go ... Thea."

A second flash showed them again to the listener. Tranter was

13

still holding her away from him. In that vivid fraction of a second the agony of her face was terrible.

"Thea!" she echoed pitifully. "Ah, yes—call me Thea! Poor Thea! Oh, doesn't that name awaken ... something? Hasn't it still some charm? Once you said it was the only name in all the world. Is it nothing to you now?"

"Nothing," he answered.

In spite of his resistance she was forcing herself nearer to him. The magic of her presence was binding him.

"Am I less beautiful?" she whispered. "Have I lost anything that used to draw you? Is not my hair as golden? Are not my eyes as bright—my lips as red? Am I not as soft to touch? Where could you find anything better than me?"

"Keep back!" he muttered.

Her hands were about him. In the darkness he could feel the deadly loveliness of her face almost touching his own. He was yielding, inch by inch. The warmth of her breath ... the perfume of her body.... Her closeness was intoxicating—maddening.

"Oh, let me come to you," she prayed. "I will follow you barefooted to the end of the world. I will live for you—slave for you—die for you. Only let me come. Let me leave all this—and come to you ... to-morrow...."

A groan was wrung from him. He crushed her to him.

"Come then!" he cried desperately. "Come, if you will!..."

A vivid flash, which seemed to burst almost over their heads, showed them locked in each other's arms, their lips pressed together.

Monsieur Dupont raised himself quickly. There was the sound of running footsteps on the path behind him. Monsieur Dupont had just time to turn the corner before the disordered figure of the theatrical manager loomed up before him.

"The madman is in the garden! He ran this way."

"Diable!" said Monsieur Dupont.

"I found him sneaking towards the house. He bolted out here."

Unaccustomed to physical exertion, the manager laid a heavy hand on Monsieur Dupont's shoulder, and mopped his forehead breathlessly.

"The scoundrel means mischief," he declared. "He must be found."

"Where is Mr. Copplestone?"

"I called him, but couldn't get an answer. He must be away at the other end of the garden."

"No one has passed this way," Monsieur Dupont assured him. "For a half-hour I have been wandering about these horrible paths."

14

"It's a devil of a garden," the manager admitted. "The fellow won't get very far. Let's look about here."

Fortified with a fresh supply of breath, he released Monsieur Dupont's shoulder, and made a brisk movement towards the direction from which the Frenchman had come.

Monsieur Dupont blocked the way.

"No, no—it would be a waste of time. I have come from there."

"To the river, then," the manager cried, bearing him round. "He may be trying to get across."

He was evidently familiar with the intricacies of the garden. In a few minutes, after a dozen turnings, they reached the gleam of water.

"Keep your eyes open for the next flash," the manager directed.

He peered about. A moment later the lightning lit up the calm stretch of the river and the broad lawns sloping down to it. Monsieur Dupont detected no form or movement—but with a startling shout, the manager bounded away from him across the lawns.

Monsieur Dupont blinked after him in astonishment.

He was alone again—in a new and even darker part of the endless garden.

Chapter IV

Destruction

A deep-toned clock in the house struck twelve.

Rain began to fall. A few moments later the financier hurried across the lawns with his collar turned up. The danseuse followed him. She seemed a disappointed and indignant woman.

"It's almost an insult," she complained overtaking him.

"Noth a penny more," said the financier firmly.

They both turned quickly. Her hand gripped his arm convulsively. Wild shouting arose in the darkness, and the sound of someone forcing a headlong way through hedge and bush.

The Reverend Percival Delamere was rushing towards the house as if the entire penalties of sin were at his heels.

"A corpse! A corpse by the river! Miss Manderson has been murdered!"

The danseuse uttered a terrified cry. The financier shook.

"Murderedth?" he gasped, shrinking back.

The clergyman was shattered by horror.

"By the river ... almost torn to pieces...."

The danseuse screamed loudly. A figure bounded up behind them, and a hand seized the clergyman's throat in a savage grip. The furious, distorted face of George Copplestone glared down at him. He struggled, freeing himself with all his strength.

"Copplestone," he choked, "something dreadful has happened to Miss Manderson. I found her by the river ... horribly torn...."

From another direction, Tranter reached them, breathless.

"What is the matter? What has happened?"

The financier clung to him.

"Mith Manderthon ... murderedth."

Tranter shook him off, and stood very still. The agony on his face passed unnoticed. As the theatrical manager and Mrs. Astley-Rolfe arrived at a run, Copplestone, with a sound like the cry of a raging animal, grasped the unhappy clergyman by the arm, and dashed off towards the river.

The others followed. They found her lying a few yards from the water's edge. The manager struck a match, and they looked down.

The danseuse shrieked, and fainted. Mrs. Astley-Rolfe sank on her knees, sobbing, and covered her face with her hands. The financier sickened, and turned away, trembling violently.

"God!" Tranter cried—"some one must have stamped on her!"

He bent down. "Thea...." he whispered.

Something like a sob shook him. But the others did not see.

"It must have been a wild beast," shuddered the clergyman.

"It is the work of a madman," said the manager hoarsely. "He has utterly destroyed her—as he threatened."

George Copplestone stood without a tremor. As he looked down at the broken form all his frenzy disappeared. The distortion of his first fury faded from his face, leaving it set in a pallid, lifeless mask. He contemplated the dreadful destruction at his feet without a sign of horror, or even of pity. He was perfectly steady. Not a quiver escaped him. Stooping down, he asked quietly for assistance to carry the body to the house.

"Wait a bit," said the manager, looking at him curiously. "She ought not to be moved before the police come."

Copplestone straightened himself, and remained silent.

"Let Gluckstein take the women in, and telephone to the Police Station," the manager suggested.

Mrs. Astley-Rolfe raised her bloodless face.

"Yes, yes," she sobbed. "Let me go. It's too horrible. I can't bear it."

Tranter raised her up. The danseuse had recovered consciousness, and was crying hysterically. Suddenly the financier startled them in a thin high voice, pointing a shaking finger into the darkness.

"Someone ith moving! Out there behind uth! Whoth there? Whoth there?"

They swung round, straining their eyes into the blackness.

"Who's there?" the manager called.

An answering voice reached them. The manager struck another match. On the edge of the darkness they saw an enormous figure.

"It's Monsieur Dupont!" Tranter cried.

"My friends," exclaimed Monsieur Dupont, "at last I find you! What is the matter?"

Copplestone looked at him steadily.

"The matter," he said evenly, "is that Miss Manderson has been murdered."

Monsieur Dupont uttered an extraordinary exclamation. He was instantly galvanized into a condition of seething energy. With what was almost a snarl, he brushed the financier aside, and reached the white mangled form on the ground.

For a tense minute he knelt beside it. The others waited.

"Destroyed," they heard him mutter—"utterly destroyed...."

17

When he rose, his eyes were full of tears.

"It is terrible. Who was with her last?"

"I was with her less than a quarter of an hour ago," Tranter replied. "She said she was going back to the house, and asked me to find Mr. Copplestone, and tell him that she was not feeling well."

"Where are your police?" asked Monsieur Dupont.

"Gluckstein is going to take the ladies back to the house, and telephone for them," the manager returned.

The financier departed with his charges. The four men remained, facing each other over the dead body. Rain was falling heavily.

"Poor girl," said the clergyman huskily.

"That such a brute should be at large," the manager added.

Copplestone's gaze again became rivetted to the ground. He seemed unconscious of their presence. He was like a man alone and dazed in a strange world.

Then the storm burst over them with all its fury. The rain poured down in torrents, the lightning was incessant. It was as if the elements themselves, in their rage, were seeking to complete the work of destruction.

"We can't leave her out in this—police or no police," the clergyman shivered.

Copplestone bent down again. The manager moved to assist, but Tranter put him aside, and assisted Copplestone to lift the ghastly burden in his arms. Then they picked their way slowly along the winding paths to the house.

When they entered the decorated room, Copplestone's strange immobility flashed upon him with startling suddenness. Uttering a oath, he placed what he had previously been carrying with dull indifference roughly on a couch, and hurled himself furiously upon the confusion of decorations, tearing and crushing everything into a smashed heap on the floor. So overwhelming was his violence that no one dared attempt to stop him. He dashed the lights to the ground, and rent the flags with appalling ferocity. In a few moments a shattered pile was all that remained of the medley of illumination. He stood on the pile and ground his heels into it.

Then all the energy was snuffed out of him like the switching off of an electric current. The dull heavy cloud descended on him again. He stared vacantly at the others, shrugged his shoulders slightly, and turned his back on them.

The silence remained unbroken until a loud ringing at the front door bell announced the arrival of the police.

Chapter V

Copplestone

Detective-Inspector Fay was an able and successful officer, of international reputation, whose achievements had placed a substantial price on his head in most countries sufficiently civilized to possess their criminal organizations. His bag had included many famous law-breakers, and, though now employed in less strenuous directions, he was admitted to be one of the most skilful and reliable of Scotland Yard's unravelers of mystery. But, experienced as he was, the inspector could not suppress his horror and indignation when the mutilated body of Christine Manderson was uncovered to him.

"What, in God's name, was there in this garden to-night?" he demanded, shuddering.

"A madman," the theatrical manager muttered.

The inspector's glance rested on him for an instant, but passed on. He made no further remarks during his examination—but when, concluding it, he carefully replaced the covering and turned again to the others, there was a concentrated gleam in his eyes and a certain set to his face that were known to bode ill to the perpetrators of the deeds that inspired them.

"There can scarcely be a whole bone in her body," he declared, regarding them all intently. "Her face is smashed to pulp; some of the hair has been wrenched from her head; and even the bones of her fingers are broken. It is the most brutal and disgusting crime I have had the misfortune to meet with in the whole of my thirty years experience."

He gave a brief order to an attendant constable, who moved to the door.

"If you will kindly retire with the constable to the next room," he requested, "I will take a separate account from every one. Perhaps Mr. Copplestone will give me his information first."

The constable marshalled them into an adjoining room, which the danseuse filled with complaints at this prolonged detention. Copplestone remained behind. His dullness and immobility had increased almost to a stupor.

"She was engaged to marry me," he said, in a slow lifeless tone, "since yesterday."

Inspector Fay seated himself at a table, and opened his note-book.

"We fully sympathize with you, Mr. Copplestone," he said quietly, "and I am afraid it is poor consolation to promise you that justice shall be done on the inhuman criminal, whoever it may be."

"Justice?" Copplestone returned, in the same weary, monotonous voice. "Of what use is Justice? Can it call her back—or mend her broken body?"

"Unfortunately, it cannot," the inspector admitted. "But it is all humanity can do. Will you answer a few questions, as clearly and briefly as possible? The great thing in a case like this is to lose no time at the beginning."

Copplestone sat down, and passed an unsteady hand across his forehead.

"Go on," he said dully.

"Where and when did you first meet Miss Manderson?"

"She came over from New York two months ago, to play in a new piece at the Imperial. I have an interest in the theater, and saw her there for the first time about a week after her arrival."

"Do you know anything of her life and associations in America?"

"Very little. She was not communicative. She only told me a few of her theatrical experiences."

"So far as you know," the inspector proceeded, "had she an enemy in this country—or was there any one who could have wished to harm her?"

"Apparently there was," Copplestone returned. "I did not know it until to-night."

Mechanically, in the manner of one repeating a lesson, he described the visit of the young millionaire, and his threat against Christine Manderson.

"And the name of this young man?" the inspector asked, bending over his note-book.

"James Layton."

Inspector Fay looked up sharply.

"Layton? The man they call the Mad Philanthropist?"

"I don't know," Copplestone replied wearily. "He may be."

"James Layton is very well known to us," the inspector said slowly. "He is a charitable fanatic, who does more good in the East End than all the Royally Patronized Associations put together. But how in the world did he come to know Miss Manderson?"

"She never mentioned him to me," Copplestone stated. "I had not heard of him until he burst into this house to-night."

The inspector made several notes.

"He has educated and trained as his assistant a particularly wild specimen of a coster girl, who is madly in love with him...." He closed his note-book with a snap. "You say the words he used were that rather than allow Miss Manderson to become engaged to you, he would tear her to pieces with his own hands, and utterly destroy her?"

"So they told me," Copplestone answered heavily. "I was not in the room. I refused to see him."

"And he left quite quietly?"

"Yes."

"Did Miss Manderson show any particular fear of the threat?"

"She was very much upset, and fainted when she came into the room. I should have sent for the police at once, but she begged me not to, and insisted that he didn't mean what he said. I wish to God I hadn't listened."

"So there was no doubt that she knew him?"

"No. She certainly knew him."

"Afterwards, you say, he was seen in the garden when you were all out after dinner?" the inspector continued.

"Yes."

"Who saw him?"

"Mr. Bolsover, the theatrical manager, found him sneaking about the house, and chased him out in the direction of the crime."

"Did any one see him, besides Mr. Bolsover?"

"Apparently not. He says he called to me—but I had gone into the house to fill my cigarette-case, and did not hear him."

"He escaped from Mr. Bolsover, and was not seen again?"

"Yes."

"Was there any one else," the inspector asked slowly, "who might, for any reason, have entertained unfriendly feelings towards Miss Manderson?"

Copplestone's glance sharpened a little under the question.

"I suppose there was," he admitted, with some reluctance.

"Who was it?"

Copplestone paused, frowning.

"Please do not hesitate," the inspector pressed firmly. "We must know everything."

"Perhaps," the tired voice confessed, "it wasn't altogether playing the game to announce my engagement so unexpectedly to—to——"

"Well?" the inspector insisted—"to whom?"

"To Phyllis Astley-Rolfe."

There was silence for a moment. The inspector waited quietly. With an effort, Copplestone continued.

"I am afraid it was rather cruel. She'd annoyed me lately, and I put up some decorations, and announced the news in a dramatic

21

way ... to mock her." He broke off, staring at the remains of the decorations on the floor. "But I tore them down. I shall never decorate again...."

The inspector watched him closely. He seemed to be on the verge of sleep.

"Then Mrs. Astley-Rolfe had reason to be jealous of Miss Manderson?" the inspector demanded briskly.

"I suppose ... she had."

"Good reason?"

"Possibly."

"Had you given her definite cause to believe that you intended to ask her to marry you?"

"Perhaps so. At any rate ... I had not given her definite cause to believe that I didn't."

His voice sank to a whisper. He leant back limply in his chair.

"There is only one more question I need trouble you with at present," the inspector said. "Who was the last person to be with Miss Manderson before the crime was discovered?"

Copplestone scarcely opened his eyes.

"Mr. Tranter was with her near the river. She left him to go back to the house, and asked him to find me, and tell me she was not well."

"Did he find you?"

"Yes. And I at once went into the house."

"Where were you when Mr. Tranter found you?"

"I was crossing the second lawn—towards the tennis courts."

The inspector was busy with his note-book.

"Were you alone?"

"Yes. I had just come out of the house after filling my cigarette-case, as I told you. I was looking for Miss Manderson, and wondering where she had got to. If only I had gone in the right direction ... I might have been in time...."

"After Mr. Tranter had spoken to you, you say you went into the house at once?"

"At once. I waited nearly ten minutes for her, and came out again just as Mr. Delamere gave the alarm. I'm afraid I handled him roughly...."

The words trailed off into silence. A convulsive shudder passed through him.

"Then we all ran off ... to where she lay," his voice shook. "Something seemed to give way ... here...." he pressed his hands to his head. "Is there ... anything more ... you want to know?"

The inspector rose.

"Only one thing. Will you kindly give me the names of your guests in the other room?"

Copplestone complied slowly. Inspector Fay wrote the names down.

"Thank you," he said, laying down his book. "I am sorry to have had to give you the pain of answering so many questions. I am afraid you are quite overwrought. I should advise you to try to get some sleep."

"Sleep," Copplestone murmured, rising weakly from his chair. "Sleep.... Good God."

The inspector himself made a gesture of fatigue.

"I only got back from another heavy case as your message came in," he apologized, stifling a yawn. "Tobacco is the only thing that keeps me going. Could you give me a cigarette?"

Without answering, Copplestone languidly produced an elaborately jeweled gold cigarette-case, and handed it to the inspector.

There were two cigarettes in it.

Inspector Fay took one, with a perfectly impassive countenance, and returned the case. Copplestone replaced it in his pocket.

"Please give whatever instructions you like to my man," he said dully—"and let me know if you want me. I shall be in my room."

He turned, and moved away with slow heavy steps, disappearing between the same curtains through which, a few hours before, he had presented Christine Manderson to his guests.

The inspector stood looking after him, fingering the cigarette thoughtfully, a very curious expression on his face. He showed no further signs of fatigue.

"I wonder why you lied to me," he muttered—and laid the cigarette on the table.

He glanced down the list of names, and went to the door. The constable had mounted guard over his prisoners with extraordinary dignity. The voice of the danseuse was still raised in lamentation.

"Monsieur Dupont," the inspector called.

The constable passed on the summons—and Monsieur Dupont instantly obeyed it.

Chapter VI

The Trail Of Corpses

The inspector closed the door behind him. "What has brought you back into the arena?" he asked quietly.

"A riddle," the Frenchman answered, in an equally low tone.

"It must have been something pretty big to have tempted you," the inspector remarked, coming closer to him.

"It was," Monsieur Dupont admitted.

The other glanced cautiously towards the curtains at the far end of the room.

"Why are you here—in this house?" he demanded softly.

"By chance," Monsieur Dupont replied.

"Did you know Copplestone before?"

"I did not. I had never seen him. I came with my friend, Tranter."

"You were here all the evening?"

"Yes."

"Anything to tell me?" the inspector asked, looking at him intently.

Monsieur Dupont smiled.

"Only, my friend, that I imagine you will find it an interesting and somewhat unusual case."

"That's not enough—from you," the inspector retorted.

"If I may be permitted to advise—it is a case in which you would do well to ignore the obvious."

"I want more than that," insisted the inspector.

The huge Frenchman remained silent.

"You are not a man to waste your time on this kind of entertainment," said the inspector slowly. "Is there any connection between the crime to-night, and your so-called 'riddle'?"

"The connection of death," said Monsieur Dupont.

There was something of awe in his voice and manner.

"For two years," he said, "I have been following in the track of something, which, in the words of our great Dumas—'must have passed this way, for I see a corpse.'"

"That quotation referred to a woman," said the inspector quickly.

"From me," returned Monsieur Dupont evenly, "it is sexless—at present."

The inspector frowned.

"Come," he said impatiently—"in what way are you mixed up in this?"

"In the way of my quotation—a corpse. I started my quest two years ago—over a dead body, torn and mutilated. At the end of the first year I found another dead body, torn and mutilated. I follow on and on—from one point to the next point—often with no more than the instinct of the hunter to guide me. And here, at the end of the second year, there is yet another dead body, torn and mutilated. It is horrible. I sicken. I wish I had remained in my retirement."

"What were the two previous crimes?" the inspector asked.

"Two women—two very beautiful women."

Inspector Fay started, staring at him.

"Miss Manderson was a beautiful woman," he said slowly.

Monsieur Dupont's enormous head nodded several times.

"She was," he agreed deliberately. "The most beautiful of the three."

There was silence for a moment. Then the inspector laid a hand on the Frenchman's shoulder.

"We have worked together a good many times in the past," he said, with more cordiality than before.

"We have, indeed," Monsieur Dupont responded pleasantly.

"And though your methods were always fanciful compared with our's, I know enough of your powers to ask you a simple, straight question."

"I am at your service," said Monsieur Dupont.

"You were here on the spot when this crime was committed. Who, or what, smashed the body of that unfortunate woman to pulp in this garden to-night?"

Monsieur Dupont's gigantic form seemed to acquire a new, strange dignity—a solemnity—as though he were in the presence, or speaking, of something before which humanity must bow its head.

"A Destroyer," he whispered. "A Destroyer who strikes with neither fear nor compunction—and passes on without pity or remorse. A Destroyer who is as old as the sins of men, and as young as the futures of their children."

"You always spoke in parables," the inspector exclaimed irritably. "What do you mean?"

"I mean," said Monsieur Dupont, "that I believe the thing which passed through this crooked garden to-night, leaving death so horribly behind it, is the same thing that has already passed on twice before me, and left the same death in its wake. I cannot tell you any more. Let us both go our own ways, as we have done so many times before. I do not wish to take any credit in this affair. If I am able to prove its connection with my own case, and to solve it, I shall hand the whole matter over to you."

25

The inspector appeared somewhat relieved.

Monsieur Dupont's eyes were fixed on an unframed photograph of Christine Manderson, which stood on a small cabinet in front of him.

"Please compound a felony," he said softly—and slipped it into his pocket.

"Where are you to be found?" the inspector asked.

"At the Hotel Savoy." He yawned. "I am very sleepy," he complained. "If you will finish with Mr. Tranter as soon as possible, he will take me back in his car."

He turned to the door.

"Stay," said the inspector.

He stopped.

"You have not lost your old fantastic kink," said the inspector, with a faint smile. "The last time we ran together you were five minutes ahead of me at the finish. This time—we will see who is the first to pass the post."

"My friend," said Monsieur Dupont, "I will do my best to give you a good race."

He passed out of the room. The inspector followed him to the door, and called for Mr. Tranter.

Chapter VII

Tranter

"Mr. Tranter," said the inspector, "I understand that you were the last person to see Miss Manderson alive."

"I believe I was," Tranter replied.

The inspector sat down again at the table, and re-opened his note-book.

"Will you kindly tell me exactly what happened from the time you went out into the garden after dinner, and the time you left Miss Manderson?"

"We strolled away from the house together, in the direction of the river. The events of the evening seemed to have upset her very much, and she was nervous of the storm. We walked about, I should think, for nearly half an hour, until the lightning became very vivid——"

"Did you see or hear any one in that part of the garden?" the inspector interrupted.

"No. Most of the others went to the lawns, in the opposite direction. When the lightning became very vivid, Miss Manderson said she would return to the house, and asked me to go down to the lawns to find Mr. Copplestone, and send him in to her. She was obviously unwell."

"You will be able to show me the place where you left her?"

"I think so. It was very dark—but I remember that we had just passed under a number of rose-arches across the path."

"It was, I presume, further away from the house than the spot where the body was found?"

"The body was found close to the river, about half-way between the house and the place where I left her," Tranter replied.

"So we may surmise that she had got about half-way to the house before the attack was made. How far would that actually be?"

"Along those winding paths," Tranter calculated, "I should say roughly about a hundred and fifty yards."

"Did she start to walk to the house immediately you left her?"

"Yes. She started in that direction as I started in the other."

"Then," mused the inspector, "she must have met the criminal, whoever it was, at the most within three minutes of leaving you?"

"Presumably she must," Tranter agreed.

"And was that," pursued the inspector, "about the spot where she might have met the young man, Layton, who was, it appears, being chased out towards the river by Mr. Bolsover?"

"It might be. But I do not know anything about the chase. If I had known that Layton was in the garden, I should not have left her."

"Where did you find Mr. Copplestone?"

"On the lawns."

"How long after you parted from her?"

"Only a few minutes. Four or five."

"Was he alone?"

"Yes. He was looking for Miss Manderson himself. He went into the house at once."

Silence followed while the inspector added to his notes.

"Mr. Tranter," he said quietly—and his eyes rested for a moment on the cigarette on the table, "I have only one suggestion to make. You will understand that it is only a suggestion, but I want to be perfectly clear. Considering that this was the evening of Miss Manderson's engagement to Mr. Copplestone, might she not have been expected to have strolled away from the house, and to have spent that following half-hour, with him rather than with you?"

Tranter hesitated.

"I suppose she might," he admitted.

The inspector was looking at him sharply.

"It is a small point," he said smoothly. "Perhaps you can clear it up."

There was another pause. Tranter was plainly embarrassed.

"Inspector," he said at last, "I must, of course, tell you everything—but I should be obliged if for obvious reasons, you will keep as much as possible to yourself."

"That, sir," returned the inspector firmly, "you must leave to my discretion."

"I am content to do so," Tranter said. "The truth is—I had met Miss Manderson before."

"Ah!" said the inspector softly.

"I knew her first nearly six years ago, in Chicago. Her real name was not Christine Manderson."

The inspector's eyes began to brighten. He turned to a fresh page in his note-book.

"She took that name, she told me to-night, when she went on the stage in New York. She was really Thea Colville."

Inspector Fay started.

"Thea Colville? The Chicago adventuress?"

"I believe some people called her that," Tranter returned shortly.

"The woman who ruined Michael Cranbourne, son of Joshua Cranbourne, the Nitrate King?"

28

"She had finished with Cranbourne before I knew her," Tranter replied. "He was a scoundrel. Whatever happened, she certainly could not be blamed."

The inspector was making rapid notes.

"She was not so wild as she was painted," Tranter continued. "Women with such beauty as hers have a thousand temptations. The sins of a beautiful woman are always many degrees blacker than the sins of a plain one. We became very intimate—and I am afraid I allowed her to expect more from me than I actually intended. I was called back to England unexpectedly, and heard nothing more of her until Mr. Copplestone brought her into this room to-night."

He stopped. Emotion had crept into his voice.

"During the most part of your conversation with her, were you walking about, or standing still?"

"Standing still."

"You have said that you did not hear any one moving about near you while you were speaking to her?"

"No."

"Were there trees or hedges about, where some one might have hidden to overhear you?"

"There was a hedge," Tranter replied. "But I did not notice the spot particularly."

"You will be able to point it out to me to-morrow."

"I think so. As I say, I did not particularly notice it—and the possibility of being overheard certainly did not occur to me. I am afraid at that moment caution was hardly a consideration with either of us."

The inspector closed his note-book.

"Unless circumstances compel me to do otherwise," he promised, "I will keep your story to myself. Will you tell me whether the announcement of Mr. Copplestone's engagement to Miss Manderson produced a noticeable effect on any particular person in the room? Please do not hesitate to answer."

"It certainly appeared to be unwelcome news to Mrs. Astley-Rolfe," Tranter replied, "but she very quickly recovered herself."

"It seemed, in fact, to be a considerable shock to her?"

"Yes."

"Were you in the room when this young man, James Layton, burst in?"

"I was. Monsieur Dupont and I had just arrived."

"It is true that he said that rather than allow Miss Manderson to become engaged to Mr. Copplestone, he would tear her to pieces with his own hands?"

"Those were his exact words."

The inspector rose.

"I understand that you brought Monsieur Dupont here with you as your friend?" he remarked casually.

"Yes. He only arrived in London last night."

"Do you know him well?"

"Fairly," Tranter replied. "I am under a great obligation to him. He saved my life in Paris, a year ago."

"Has he mentioned anything of the business that has brought him to this country?" the inspector asked, moving to the door.

"Only that he had come to solve a strange riddle."

A faint, rather grim smile passed over the inspector's face.

"I am obliged to you, sir," he said, opening the door. "If you will kindly return here at ten o'clock in the morning—and bring Monsieur Dupont with you—I shall ask you to show me the various places you have referred to in the garden."

When Tranter returned to the waiting-room, he found Monsieur Dupont asleep in an armchair. The room was very quiet. The danseuse had subsided into an interim condition of mute tension. Mrs. Astley-Rolfe was deathly white, but perfectly composed. The men made occasional remarks to each other.

"Mrs. Astley-Rolfe," the inspector called.

Chapter VIII

Mrs. Astley-Rolfe

"Madam," said the inspector, placing a chair for her, "I need only trouble you with one or two questions. You will understand that it is necessary for me to account for each member of this party, so that I may know which of them can, or cannot, assist me in my investigations."

She sat down with a weary movement. Her hands trembled slightly.

"It is very dreadful," she shuddered. "Such a frightful crime is inconceivable. Who could have hated the poor girl so dreadfully?"

"That remains to be discovered," the inspector returned quietly. "I have no doubt we shall succeed in clearing it up."

"I hope you will," she said fervently. "Please ask me any questions you like."

The inspector kept his eyes fixed on his note-book.

"You went into the garden with the others after dinner?"

"Yes."

"Will you please tell me with whom, and in what part of the garden, you passed the time before the crime was discovered?"

"I was alone," she said slowly.

"The whole time?"

"Yes. I was not feeling very well, and did not want the trouble of talking. I walked away by myself."

"You know the way about the garden quite well?"

"Quite."

"In what direction did you walk?"

"To the croquet lawn."

"Did you see anything of the others?"

"No."

"Or hear any voices?"

"No."

"Nothing until the alarm was given?"

"Nothing. It was an isolated part of the garden. When I heard Mr. Delamere shouting, I ran back to the house, and found them on the lawn."

The inspector shot a keen glance at her.

"Did you know Miss Manderson well?"

"I had only met her three or four times."

"I suppose—being one of the most beautiful women on the American stage, and about to appear for the first time in London— you heard her a good deal talked about?"

"Yes." Her voice was just perceptibly harder. "People were taking great interest in her."

"Did you hear her private affairs, and mode of life, discussed at any time?"

"No."

"Or the name of James Layton, the millionaire philanthropist, mentioned in conjunction with her's?"

"Never."

"Thank you, madam. I need not trouble you any further. Will you kindly leave me your address, in case I should have to ask you for any more information?"

He wrote the address down, and bowed her out.

Chapter IX

The Danseuse

"Madame Krashoff," summoned the inspector.

The danseuse was in a condition of the utmost distress.

"Mon Dieu! Mon Dieu!" she wept.

"Please calm yourself, madame," the inspector requested patiently.

"I ken nothin' o' the creeme!" she sobbed thoughtlessly.

"I am sure of that," he declared gravely. "I merely wish to establish the movements of every one here. With whom did you pass the time after you went out into the garden until the alarm was given?"

"Wi' M'soo Gluckstein," she whimpered.

"All the time?"

"N-no."

"How much of the time?"

She became more collected.

"He said to me something that made me angry," she replied, with a touch of viciousness. "I walk away from him. Then it rain, and I overtook him as I go back to the house."

"How long were you away from him?" the inspector asked.

"Ma foi, I cannot tell. Maybe ten minutes."

"Did you see any one else?"

"No."

"In what part of the garden were you when you left him?"

"Behind the tennis courts."

"That is some way from the river?"

"Yes, yes—ver' far away."

"Thank you, madame."

Chapter X

Mr. Gluckstein

The financier was extremely agitated, and tried to shake hands with the inspector.

"Mr. Gluckstein, I understand from Madame Krashoff that you were with her in the garden for the greater part of the time before the crime was discovered."

"I wath," the financier quivered—"indeed I wath, inthpector."

"Then she left you for about ten minutes?"

"Not tho much ath ten minutes," corrected the financier hastily.

"What did you do after she left you?"

"I stayed vere I vath—until the rain commenthed."

"Did you see any one else?"

"No one at allth."

"Thank you," said the inspector. "Please leave me your address, in case I should want to ask you any further questions."

The financier produced a card with trembling fingers.

Chapter XI

The Clergyman

"Mr. Delamere," said the inspector, "you discovered the body?"

"I did," replied the clergyman, with a shiver.

"Were you alone when you found it?"

"Yes. I had been walking with Mr. Bolsover for about quarter of an hour. Then he turned back to find some of the others, and I strolled on to the river."

"Did you meet any one else?"

"No."

"You saw nothing of this young man, Layton, who was chased towards the river by Mr. Bolsover?"

"Nothing whatever."

"No sounds of a struggle?"

"No. I heard nothing."

"Was the body lying in your path?"

"No. Some distance aside. I saw something white on the ground in one of the lightning flashes, and went to see what it was."

"I shall have to ask you to return here at ten o'clock, to show me the exact spot."

"Certainly."

"Thank you, Mr. Delamere."

Chapter XII

Mr. Bolsolver

"My God!" exclaimed the manager, "what an appalling business!"

"It is," the inspector agreed shortly.

"She was to have appeared at my theater, too," said the manager ruefully.

"I understand that you found Layton sneaking about the house?"

"Yes. I first strolled out with Mr. Delamere. Then I left him, and went back to see where the others had got to, and saw Layton creeping round the side of the house towards the open drawing-room windows. He heard my footsteps on the path, and bolted."

"To the river?"

"Yes. I shouted for Mr. Copplestone, but there was no answer—so I followed him."

"You are quite certain it was Layton?"

"Perfectly. I saw his face in the light of the windows, and he was wearing the peculiar kind of slouch hat he had carried when he came into the room."

"Apparently no one saw him in the garden except yourself."

"Unfortunately not. I met the Frenchman, Monsieur Dupont, a little way from the river—but he had not seen him."

"It was a pity you did not manage to catch him," the inspector remarked.

"Confound it, yes! But it was easy to get away in such a garden as this. There wasn't a chance of finding him."

"What did you do, after meeting Monsieur Dupont?"

"We went on to the river together. I thought I saw a movement among the trees when the lightning lit them up—but there was nothing. I walked round about there for a few minutes, and then went back to warn Copplestone."

"Leaving Monsieur Dupont by the river?"

"Yes. Before I reached the house, I heard Mr. Delamere shouting the alarm."

"Thank you," said the inspector, closing his note-book. "I am afraid I shall have to trouble you to come here at ten o'clock and show me certain places in the garden."

"I am entirely at your disposal," said the manager.

He went out. The inspector sat down at the table, and remained perfectly still for half an hour.

Chapter XIII

The Trinity of Death

In Tranter's car, its owner and Monsieur Dupont started, at half-past one, on their return from the crooked house.

The storm had passed, and the air was fresh and cool. It was possibly the atmospheric clearance which accounted for the fact, that, however, fatigued he had been, or appeared to be, at the end of his conversation with the inspector, Monsieur Dupont was now particularly wide-awake and alert.

"Dieu!" he cried, "what a terrible crime! Almost to tear that woman to pieces—to crush her—to rend her! And what a woman! Ma foi, what a woman!"

There was a pause. Monsieur Dupont accepted and lit a cigar from Tranter's case.

"My friend," he said quietly, "I wish to be quite fair to you."

"Fair to me?" Tranter echoed, surprised.

"Something happened to-night which you doubtless believe to be unknown to every one except yourself."

Tranter turned to him quickly.

"I have not the habit," Monsieur Dupont continued, "of listening to private conversations between other people. It is only on very rare occasions that I have done so. I did so to-night."

"What do you mean?" Tranter exclaimed.

"In that horrible garden, before the crime was committed," pursued Monsieur Dupont evenly, "I lost my way. Such a garden must have been especially designed to cause innocent people to lose their way. I wandered about. How I wandered!"

"What did you overhear?" asked Tranter, in a strained voice.

"A conversation—between that unfortunate Mademoiselle Manderson, and yourself."

"You heard it?" Tranter cried sharply.

"I heard it," admitted Monsieur Dupont. "I heard a great part of it. I believe nearly all. I should not have done so. Understand, I make you all my apologies. It was improper to listen. But the storm, the surroundings, the scene itself, excited me. I listened."

Tranter remained silent.

"I continued to listen, until Mr. Bolsover found me. He was following that young man, Layton. I went with him to the river."

Tranter was still silent—staring straight in front of him with fixed eyes.

"You saw a picture of weakness," he said, at last. "I am not proud of it. I should much prefer to be able to think that no one had seen it. I gave Inspector Fay an account of the whole scene, and of my previous acquaintance with Christine Manderson. He promised to keep it to himself. I hope you will do the same."

"I shall indeed," the other assured him.

"I am only human," Tranter went on, with an effort—"more human than I thought. I resisted her once by taking flight. I couldn't resist her to-night."

He mastered his emotion.

"From the moment she first came into the room I was helpless. I knew what would come of it—but I couldn't tear myself away. It was the whole spell—with all the new strength of memories. I knew she intended to find me alone in the garden." He paused. "I had to let her."

"Human nature," said Monsieur Dupont consolingly, "is human nature."

Silence followed. Monsieur Dupont thoughtfully puffed at his cigar.

"A crooked house in a crooked garden," he said, at length, "is a combination from which all honest people should shrink. Those who frequent it must be, for the most part, crooked people. They were, for the most part, crooked people to-night."

"It was a crooked evening from beginning to end," Tranter said wearily.

"It was a wicked evening," Monsieur Dupont declared—"full of wicked thoughts. A crime was the natural and logical end to such an evening. It would have been surprising if there had not been one."

He smoked vigorously for some moments—then made an expansive gesture.

"Are there not," he demanded, "houses and gardens and thunder-storms that awaken cruel and shameful impulses that would never be aroused in other houses and other gardens and other storms? Does not the influence of good and noble decorations uplift us to joy and patriotism? Why should not the influence of mean and sinful decorations degrade us to murder and destruction? The flags that fly over the innocent revels of children are innocent flags, and inspire kind feelings and happiness. But remove the same flags to a Bull-ring, and they become evil flags, inspiring lust for the blood and slaughter of helpless creatures—the basest of human instincts."

"You are fantastic," said Tranter, with a gloomy smile.

"In fantasy," returned Monsieur Dupont, "are the world's greatest truths."

He carefully deposed the ash from his cigar.

"Will you please tell me," he went on, "something more about our strange host to-night—the man who chooses so much crookedness to live in, when there is straightness to be had for the same price?"

"I know very little more about him than I told you last night," Tranter replied. "He is wealthy, and very eccentric. He seems to pass his life in a perpetual effort to be different from other people."

"He is more than eccentric," Monsieur Dupont stated. "He is mad. In a few years he will be a dangerous lunatic. And the Good God only knows what he may make of himself in the meantime."

"There are plenty of strange stories about him," Tranter said. "But I have always looked on them as greatly exaggerated."

"Probably," Monsieur Dupont remarked, "they were true."

"Whatever his reputation may be, women seem very ready to put up with his eccentricities, or pander to them, in return, no doubt, for big inroads into his banking account. He is very free with his money where the opposite sex is concerned."

"It is always so," said Monsieur Dupont, "with such men."

"He mixes chiefly in theatrical and bohemian circles—and often by no means the most desirable of those. The better people look askance on him—but he is supremely indifferent to the opinions of others, and to all the conventions. Whatever he takes it into his head to do he does, quite regardless of the approval or disapproval of other people. He is certainly not a man I would introduce to any woman who possessed even the smallest degree of physical attraction. He is supposed to be quite unscrupulous in the attainment of his objects."

"Most of us are," said Monsieur Dupont. "But we dislike to admit it."

He looked steadily out of the window for a moment.

"I wonder," he said, turning back, "what he does with the rest of that house."

"The rest of the house?" Tranter repeated.

"It is very large," said Monsieur Dupont. "It is large enough for twenty men."

"In this country," Tranter smiled, "there is no law against one man living in a house large enough for twenty, if he chooses."

"When only a small part of a house is used for ordinary purposes," remarked Monsieur Dupont, "the remainder is often used for extraordinary ones."

"You know as much of the house as I do," Tranter returned.

"As a practical man," Monsieur Dupont continued, "you may smile when I speak of such a thing as 'psychic intuition.' But you may smile, and again you may smile. I possess that intuition strongly. It has been of great use to me. The moment I entered that house to-night, I knew it was a house of sin. I knew there were hidden things in it—things that were not for honest eyes to see. I do not say—at present—that they have any connection with the crime. But they are there."

"I do not smile at such instincts," Tranter said. "I quite admit that there is a strange, uncanny atmosphere about the place. And if there are secrets in it, I am equally ready to admit that they are probably bad ones."

"They are bad ones," declared Monsieur Dupont. "They could not be anything but bad ones. When that excellent Inspector Fay has solved the mystery of the garden, he would be wise to turn his attention to the secrets of the house."

There was a pause.

"Did Layton kill her?" Tranter asked suddenly.

Monsieur Dupont shrugged his shoulders.

"The evidence is against him," he replied judicially. "Your Coroner's jury will find him guilty, and the police will not look further. They will build up a strong case. They will doubtless find that he was cruelly treated by that poor girl, and was furious to know that she was engaged to another man. He threatened, in the presence of many witnesses, to kill her in a horrible way. He was seen later in the garden, and afterwards she was found—killed in exactly that horrible way. Who would not say that in his rage and jealousy he had fulfilled his threat? Every one will be perfectly satisfied. It is enough for justice if the most likely person is hanged. And, so far, he is not only the most likely, but the only, person."

"Perhaps so," Tranter acknowledged. "But—he didn't look like a murderer. He looked a good fellow. Is there no other alternative?"

"There is an alternative," said Monsieur Dupont steadily.

"There is?"

"Yes."

Monsieur Dupont smoked composedly for a minute.

"My friend," he said—"are you inclined for an adventure?"

"I am rather busy," Tranter replied. "What is it?"

"Suppose ... I were to declare to you positively that James Layton is innocent—that he did not commit that crime in the crooked garden to-night—and that I do not intend to allow him to be hanged for a crime that he did not commit—would you give a certain amount of your time to help me to save him?"

"Certainly. I will do anything I can."

"Then," said Monsieur Dupont, "I answer the question you asked a moment ago. He did not kill her."

40

"Who did?" Tranter demanded, looking at him in astonishment.

"That is another matter. It is one thing to say who did not—but quite another to say who did. That is for us to discover. There will be very little time. I think I can promise you excitement. Possibly there will be danger. You do not object to that?"

"I have faced a certain amount of danger in my time," Tranter replied.

"Good," said Monsieur Dupont. "Then we will set ourselves— quite apart from the efforts of our friend, Inspector Fay—to solve the mystery of the crooked garden. And we will not speak a word to any one of our intention."

"You seem to have some very definite ideas on the subject already," Tranter observed.

"Ah, no," demurred Monsieur Dupont—"do not credit me with the superhuman. We have a very difficult task before us."

"But what of your other object," Tranter inquired—"the 'riddle' that you came over to solve?"

"It may be," Monsieur Dupont replied carefully, "that there is some connection between my riddle and this dreadful affair to-night. At present I cannot say. Only events themselves can prove that. But that very possibility compels me to take up a peculiar attitude—unfortunately a most necessary one. If you will assist me— as I beg you to do—you must be content to follow my guidance and instructions without question, and remain, as you call it, in the dark, until the time comes for all to be told."

"You are certainly the most mysterious person I have ever met!" Tranter exclaimed.

"It is not that I have the smallest doubt of yourself or your discretion," Monsieur Dupont hastened to explain. "On the contrary. It is simply that my position at this moment is an extraordinary one, and I cannot do what would seem to be the natural and ordinary thing. Will you help me on that understanding?"

"I will help you in any case," Tranter agreed, smiling slightly at his companion's intense seriousness. "What is to be my first task?"

"Your first task," said Monsieur Dupont gravely, "is to deposit me at the Hotel Savoy, and call for me later on your way back to Richmond."

Tranter spoke some instructions through the speaking-tube to the chauffeur. When he turned again, Monsieur Dupont was asleep. He did not open his eyes again until the car stopped at the Savoy.

Entering the hotel, he ascended to his room. In it, he mixed himself a whisky-and-soda, sat down at the writing-table, and unlocked a despatch-box.

41

He took out two photographs—each of a remarkably beautiful woman.

Under one was neatly written—

Colette d'Orsel. Nice. August 1900.

And under the other—

Margaret McCall. Boston. Dec. 1910.

From his pocket he took the photograph which the inspector had allowed him to appropriate, and laid it beside the others. The face that smiled up at him was the most beautiful of the three.

He dipped a pen in the ink, and wrote under it, in the same neat handwriting—

Christine Manderson. London. July 1919

Chapter XIV

Without Trace

At ten o'clock, Tranter and Monsieur Dupont stood with Inspector Fay in the garden. The Rev. Percival Delamere joined them a few minutes later, and the theatrical manager arrived shortly afterwards. Finally, still in the same half-dazed condition, George Copplestone emerged from the house.

"Mon Dieu," Monsieur Dupont whispered quickly. "Look at that man!"

His face was white, with a sickly pasty whiteness. In the few hours that had passed he seemed to have wasted to a startling gauntness. His cheeks were drawn, his sunken eyes dull and filmy. He moved slowly and heavily, as if compelling himself under an utter weariness.

"What do you want first?" he asked the inspector curtly.

"First," replied Inspector Fay, "I want to be shown the spot where the body was found."

Copplestone led the way across the lawns. In the daylight Monsieur Dupont eagerly followed the maze of winding paths and hedges that had imprisoned him so helplessly in the darkness. It was a veritable looking-glass garden. The end of every path mocked its beginning. To reach an object it was necessary to walk away from it. To arrive at the bank of the river, Copplestone conducted his followers in the opposite direction.

"This garden might have been designed for a crime," the inspector remarked, as they turned yet another corner.

"It was," Monsieur Dupont agreed from the rear. "It was designed for the most abominable crime of making men and women go backwards instead of forwards. And last night it attained the height of its purpose."

For an instant Copplestone glanced back at him, a quickening in his dull eyes. A moment afterwards they turned a final corner, and emerged on to the broad lawns, sloping down to the edge of the river.

Copplestone halted, and looked round, measuring distances. Then he moved on, keeping close to the trees.

"About here, I think," said the clergyman, pausing.

Copplestone stopped a few paces ahead.

"It was very dark," he said, looking at the ground. "I don't think I

43

knew exactly where we were. As near as I can judge, it was just here."

"There ought to have been some sign left to mark the place when the body was taken away," the inspector said sharply.

"You will find," said the quiet voice of Monsieur Dupont, "a pencil in the ground at the exact spot. It is a useful pencil, and I should be obliged if you would kindly return it to me."

The inspector shot him a rather grim smile. All, except Copplestone, bent down to look for the sign.

"Here it is," Tranter exclaimed, pulling a pencil out of the ground. They stood aside to give the inspector room.

"The rain has washed away any traces that might have helped us," that official grumbled, after a fruitless search.

"And even if it had not," the manager observed, "you would only have found traces of all of us, as we were all here."

The inspector continued his examination. Copplestone stood apart, his eyes fixed on the river. He did not appear to be taking the slightest interest in the proceedings.

"In what position was the body lying?" the inspector asked, looking up at the clergyman.

"It was so horribly contorted that it is difficult to say in what position it was lying," the latter replied, bending down beside him. "The head, I think, lay towards the river, and the feet towards the trees."

"It was so when we came," Copplestone corroborated, without turning his head.

"There are no signs of a struggle here," said the inspector, straightening himself after another pause. "If there had been one, some of the heavier indications might have remained in spite of the rain."

"It is possible," Monsieur Dupont suggested, "that the body was carried here from the place where the struggle did take place."

"Quite possible," the inspector agreed. He turned to Tranter. "Will you show us now, Mr. Tranter, where you parted from Miss Manderson?"

"I am not familiar with the garden," Tranter replied. "I only know, as I told you last night, that we had just passed under some arches across the path. I do not know where they are."

"Mr. Copplestone will show us," said the inspector.

Copplestone started at the sound of his own name, and turned to them.

"What next?" he asked abruptly.

"The rose arches," returned the inspector.

Copplestone indicated an opening in the trees, some distance ahead of them.

"Over here," he directed, moving towards it.

There were twelve ornamental arches, overgrown with roses. Monsieur Dupont looked at the wealth of flowers almost with reverence.

"So far," he muttered, "the only innocent things I have seen in this garden."

Tranter stopped at a point where several paths intersected.

"I left her here," he said. "I went down that path to the right, which she told me would lead to the main lawns where I should be most likely to Mr. Copplestone. She said she was going straight back to the house."

"She should have taken that path," Copplestone said, turning to one in another direction. "That is the way to the house."

"Did she know the garden well?" asked the inspector.

"Perfectly well."

"Still, she might easily have taken a wrong turning in the darkness."

"She might. But it is about the straightest path in the garden. I don't think she would have made a mistake."

Slowly and carefully Inspector Fay followed the path to the house, under the guidance of Copplestone. Every yard of the way was examined, but yielded nothing. The inspector's face became darker and darker. He stopped when they turned a corner and found themselves at the house.

"She could not possibly have got so far as this before the attack was made," he said discontentedly.

"Impossible," agreed the manager. "If the murderer had killed her here, he would have left her here. He would not have taken the risk of dragging her all the way to the river."

"It seems a curious thing," the clergyman remarked, "that apparently she did not utter any cry for help."

"Ah!" said Monsieur Dupont quietly.

He looked at the clergyman with a new interest. Copplestone also glanced at him quickly.

"Even the thunder would hardly have drowned a sharp cry, and some one would surely have heard it."

"Probably she hadn't time," suggested the manager. "No doubt he sprang out and attacked her from the back. He must have been as quick as the lightning itself."

Monsieur Dupont drew Tranter aside.

"Our clerical friend does not realize the importance of his own point," he said softly. "But he has put his finger on the key to the whole mystery."

"The key?" Tranter repeated.

"If Christine Manderson had uttered a cry for help, this would have been a simple, straightforward case," said Monsieur Dupont. "In the fact that she did not lies the whole secret of the crime."

"Bolsover's reason would seem to be the obvious one," Tranter returned. "The assault must have been made so quickly that she had no time."

"Mr. Bolsover's reason is, as you say, the obvious one," admitted Monsieur Dupont. "But it is not the correct one. I have already warned Inspector Fay to disregard the obvious. If he will not take my advice, that is his affair."

"But what do you mean?" asked Tranter.

Monsieur Dupont's voice sank lower.

"Don't you see that a cry for help would have completely transformed the whole case? It would have brought it down in one crash to a human level. It is the silence—the utter, horrible silence—that makes it what it is. It is the silence——"

The inspector's voice recalled them.

"Now, Mr. Bolsover, just whereabouts was Layton when you disturbed him?"

"He was sneaking round there," the manager replied, pointing to a corner of the house, "towards the drawing-room windows."

"Which path did he run to when he saw you?"

"That one—to the river."

"Does that path communicate anywhere with the one which we presume Miss Manderson was following to the house?"

"Yes," said Copplestone.

They moved along the path indicated by the manager. It twisted about unproductively for some distance.

"How far was he in front of you?" asked the inspector.

"I don't know," confessed the manager. "I should say about ten yards when we started—but I am not much of a runner. I had lost him altogether before I got here."

They went on.

"That cursed rain," the inspector muttered.

"This is the branch that leads to the other path," said Copplestone, halting.

"And it was further along there, by that fir tree that I met Monsieur Dupont," added the manager.

"That is so," agreed Monsieur Dupont. "Layton certainly did not come beyond this point in my direction."

"By taking that branch," the inspector calculated, "he would have met Miss Manderson just at the time that the crime was committed."

"He would," said the manager.

Monsieur Dupont turned again to Tranter.

"We must be quick," he whispered, "Layton is already hanged."

"There doesn't seem to be much chance for him," returned Tranter. "It will be a very strong case. No criminal could complain at being hanged on such evidence."

"And yet," said Monsieur Dupont slowly, "so far as the actual crime is concerned, there is not a single trace. Not one single trace. Is it not extraordinary?"

He doubled his fists.

"That luck!" he ground out angrily. "Again that luck!"

"What luck?" Tranter exclaimed.

"If that most unfortunate young man had not come here and made a fool of himself last night, the police might have searched forever without finding a clue. There is no clue here. And there was the rain. The very elements sweep up after the passing of the Destroyer."

"What on earth do you mean?" Tranter cried.

"Hush!" said Monsieur Dupont.

"I am obliged to you, gentlemen," said the inspector. "Your evidence will of course be required at the inquest, of which you will receive notice. I need not detain you any longer."

The clergyman and the manager hurried away. Monsieur Dupont lingered at the inspector's side, and Tranter strolled back with Copplestone.

"Well?" queried the inspector. "Not much doubt about it, is there?"

"You have a strong case," said Monsieur Dupont. "Very strong."

"You agree with it?"

Monsieur Dupont shrugged his shoulders.

"At all events, I am not in position, at present, to contradict it."

"You will have your work cut out to build up another one," said the inspector complacently. "There isn't a trace."

"That is it," said the other sharply. "There is no trace. There is never a trace." He lowered his voice cautiously. "One point I recommend to you, as I have just recommended it to Tranter—that remark of Mr. Delamere that there was no cry for help."

"What of it?" returned the inspector.

"It is the key," said Monsieur Dupont.

He moved on abruptly, and overtook Tranter.

Chapter XV

A Builder of Men

James Layton occupied two dingy rooms, in a dilapidated house, situated between a church and a public-house, in as squalid and unwholesome a street as any in the East End of London. In them he spent such time as was left to him—and it was not much—after his active ministrations among the denizens of the miserable neighborhood. They were scantily furnished, and of comforts there were none. He denied himself anything beyond the barest necessities of existence, with the exception of a few books and pipes, which were the companions of his odd moments of leisure, and he read and smoked in a hard wicker chair, destitute even of a cushion. He ate sparingly, of food scarcely better than that on which his neighbors subsisted, and drank little. His clothes were poor, his shirts frayed, and his boots patched—and his income was a thousand pounds a week.

In his work he was unusually broad-minded and unprejudiced. He spent none of his time in efforts to lure the occupants of the public-house on his left into the church on his right. Indeed, he was an excellent customer of the former institution, and was on the best of terms with its landlord, who was an ex-pugilist after his kind. He made no discrimination in the dispensation of his charity. He worked on the principle that before he reformed a man he must feed him—so before he attempted to deal with the mind he relieved the body. He was open-handed and unsuspicious—and wonderfully beloved. There were hundreds of people in that street, and many other streets, who would gladly have laid down their lives for him—and who imposed on him shockingly day after day in the minor matters of life. The Mad Philanthropist never turned away—never refused. He was a builder of Men. No one knew, or cared, who he was or whence he came. He never gave account of himself, or spoke of his own affairs. Curiosity was the one thing he resented. He enclosed himself, so far as private matters were concerned, within the fortifications of a reserve which no one had succeeded in penetrating. Though he held a thousand confidences, he made none. In listening to the experiences of others he never referred to his own, or even hinted whether they had been sweet or bitter. He went on his silent way—and the world was the better for him.

In his bare sitting-room he sat with his face between his hands. A girl knelt on the floor beside him.

She was a remarkable girl. Wild, wayward, with all the passions—brimful with untamed vitality—incapable of the common restraints. Her face was neither beautiful, nor, perhaps, even pretty—but Diana herself might have envied the full, lithe figure, the free grace of her movements. She was the creature of her desires—knowing no laws that opposed them. A Primitive Woman, from the dawn of the world.

"Jim," she pleaded. "Jim...."

He made no movement.

"Be a man," she whispered. "Pull yourself together."

He put her away from him roughly.

"I wish you'd go," he said dully. "I don't want you here."

Her face grew whiter. Her hands crept to him again. The light of a great love was in her eyes.

"Oh, Jim," she whispered, "I know I'm not like she was. I'm not beautiful. I'm not wonderful. I haven't anything that she had. Oh, I know all that ... so well."

He uncovered his face—it was haggard and bloodless, the face of a man in the throes of a mental hell—and looked at her, almost with revulsion.

"You?" he cried harshly. "You...? You dare to name yourself to me in the same breath with her? Get up, and look at yourself!" He pointed to a cracked mirror on the mantel-piece. "Look!" he said hoarsely, thrusting her away from him again. "Do you see how coarse and heavy and rough you are? She was light and delicate—like a snowflake. She never seemed to touch the ground. Your hair is like string—your hands are large—your voice is harsh. Her hair was like silk—gold silk in the sunshine. I could see through her hands. Her voice was music. I want you to go. You are in my way."

She sprang up, raging.

"She never loved you!" she cried. "She never cared for you—or even thought of you! She wasn't fit to touch you—to look at you!"

His face was aflame.

"Stop!" he shouted.

"I hate her!" she declared fiercely. "I hate her memory! I'm glad she's dead!"

He lunged forward from his chair, and seized her. In his fury he nearly struck her.

"As God's above us," he panted, "one more word...." His rage choked him. The words jammed in his throat.

She wrenched herself free. His arms dropped to his sides. He reeled dizzily.

"You may do what you like to me," she cried passionately. "I tell you—I'm glad she's dead! She deserved to die. She was wicked and cruel. I think God Himself destroyed her."

He sank back into his chair weakly. A sob shook him.

"God did not destroy her," he said slowly. "God never destroys. He only builds. It is men and women who destroy."

There was a long silence. She came close to him again, all her anger swallowed up in a great sympathy.

"Jim," she asked softly ... "was she so much to you?"

He became suddenly rigid.

"How did you come to know her? She wasn't your sort. She couldn't have had anything in common with you. What have you to do with women like that?"

His eyes narrowed threateningly. Her questions had struck him into a new alertness. She noticed that his knees were pressed together.

"The papers said she only came to England two months ago—for the first time. It hasn't all happened since then. I know it hasn't. There must have been something else. Something before. What was it?"

He sat glaring at her—locking and unlocking his hands.

"It all happened since then," he said jerkily. "I had never seen her before. There was nothing else."

"I don't believe it, Jim," she declared. "You are hiding something."

He avoided her steady gaze.

"Believe it or not, as you like," he retorted.

"People say there is some secret in your life," she said. "I believe there is. And I believe it was her secret too."

He lunged forward again, in a fresh paroxysm of fury.

"What is it to you?" he cried shrilly—"or to any one? Why do you pry? Suppose I have my secrets. They are no concern of yours. I give away my money—my life. Isn't it enough? What would you be—what would any of them be now—but for me? I work day and night for others. Can't I keep my soul to myself?"

"Jim," she said gently, "I'm not prying. I don't want to know your secrets. I only wanted to make it lighter for you, if you'd let me."

"You can't make it lighter for me," he returned. "No one can make it lighter. I don't want to be interfered with. I want to be left alone. What right have you to try to judge me?"

"Judge you?" she echoed. "Who could want to judge you? Why, you are the noblest man in all the world. No one could do more good than you do. Every man, woman, and child here worships you, and would die for you."

50

His anger instantly subsided.

"Ah, yes!" he said greedily—"tell me that. That's what I want to hear. Tell me they worship me—that no one could do more good than I do—that men and women would die for me. Go on telling me that!"

Her voice thrilled with her love for him.

"You brought us light and life. You have raised hundreds—as you raised me—out of misery and filth. Think of all the children you have sent away from this poison into the green fields and the sunshine—who would have died."

"Yes! yes!" he cried. "Go on! Go on! All the children...."

"You are building them," she said—her whole being transformed with tenderness. "You are making them fit to be men and women. They wouldn't have been fit without you. You are teaching them how to be clean and happy. You are showing them that they needn't be the dregs of humanity—that these hovels needn't be their world. You are giving them new interests, new thoughts, new hopes. Oh, what could be more wonderful—more splendid? It is God's own work."

"Yes! yes!" he cried again. "God's work! I am doing God's work!"

He paced up and down the room eagerly—feasting on her words—drinking her praises as an exhausted man might drink an invigorating draught. He was in the grip of a feverish energy. His blood was racing.

His quick steps shook the wretched room. The floor creaked under his tread. A lamp on the table rattled. The girl watched him nervously. She put out a hand to check him, but he brushed it aside. His looks, his movements, frightened her. He seemed to be gazing out beyond the narrow walls into a space of surging memories, that sported with his reason. He muttered incoherently, oblivious of her presence. She grew frightened.

"Jim!" she cried sharply.

He started, and stopped, looking at her vacantly.

"My work," he said restlessly. "I must get on with my work. I haven't done enough ... nearly enough. I must go on building ... go on giving light."

He let her put a hand on his arm and move him gently back to his chair. He sat down, and stared at her in a dazed fashion, as one returning to consciousness.

"Why haven't you gone?" he said heavily. "I asked you to go."

"I'm not going, Jim," she returned. "I can't leave you like this. You're not fit to be left."

His face darkened again.

"I am perfectly fit to be left," he said hardly. "And I wish to be alone."

"When you are better, I'll go," she said quietly—"if you want me to."

He made a gesture of impatience.

"I am better now," he said wearily. "I am quite well. I want you to go. Why do you persist in staying when I want you to go?"

The girl's self-control deserted her. She burst into a storm of weeping.

"I won't go," she sobbed. "I won't go—because you are in trouble—and I love you. I don't care whether you want me or not. I love you."

He heard her indifferently. Neither her tears nor her passion moved him.

"Don't talk nonsense," he snapped. "Love is nothing to me. I hate the word. You might as well talk of loving the Monument as me."

"You lifted me up," she cried. "You saved my soul and body. I was lower than any of the others before you came. You taught me—and I've tried to learn your lessons. But, oh, if you didn't mean me to love you, you should have left me where I was."

"You were a good girl," he said, with tired tolerance. "You learnt well. But I didn't mean you to love me. I don't want you to love me. What I have done for you was only part of my work—like the others. I don't want any woman to love me. I tell you, I hate the word. It means nothing to me. I only want to go on...."

Her sobs ceased. She stood very still. Her face was torn, but he was not looking at her. She turned, and went slowly towards the door, her head bowed. She seemed to be shrunken and small. All her vitality had gone. She moved like an old woman, weakly.

The door opened before she reached it. Two men stood in the passage. She started back. One of them came a few paces into the room, looking at the man in the chair.

"Mr. James Layton?"

He rose unsteadily.

"Yes," he said, "I am James Layton. What do you want?"

"We are police officers, investigating the murder of Miss Christine Manderson."

The girl uttered a cry, and sprang between them.

"What do you want with him?" she demanded fiercely. "He knows nothing about it. How should he? What is it to do with him?"

The men looked at her with quick interest. But Layton silenced her with an imperative gesture.

"I am at your service," he said quietly. "What can I do for you?"

"We are instructed to ask you to be kind enough to return with us to Scotland Yard to answer a few questions that may assist the investigation of the crime."

"Certainly," Layton returned, without hesitation.

His face was perfectly calm. He showed no fear or agitation.

"We have a taxi waiting," the man said. He spoke to Layton—but he was looking at the girl.

"I will come with you at once," Layton replied.

He took up his hat and stick. The girl leant against the wall panting, a hand pressed to her heart.

"Jim," she gasped faintly. "Jim...."

He turned, with the first sign of kindness he had yet shown to her.

"Don't be frightened," he said gently. "I shall be back in an hour or so."

She clutched him desperately.

"You sha'n't go!" she cried wildly. "You sha'n't go!"

He put her aside firmly.

"Why shouldn't I go? There is nothing to be afraid of. I must help if I can."

The door closed behind them. The girl moved from the wall, and staggered to the table, leaning on it heavily. She was ashen. Her lips were gray. She heard them leave the house—heard the car start, and listened until the sound of it died away in the length of the street. Her strength failed. She sank to her knees. A moan of agony escaped her.

"For nothing...." she whispered. "Oh, God ... for nothing...."

She heard a quiet tap at the door, but could not answer. She saw the door open slowly. An enormous figure stood on the threshold.

She struggled to her feet.

"What do you want?" she murmured fearfully. "Have you come ... for me?"

The figure squeezed its way through the narrow doorway, and closed the door.

"Mademoiselle, you are a friend of Mr. James Layton, who was taken, a few minutes ago, to Scotland Yard?"

"Yes," she cried, "yes. I am his friend. What is it?"

"Before the end of the day, Mr. Layton will be detained on the charge of murder."

She screamed.

"He didn't do it! He didn't do it!"

"The evidence is strong," said the stranger. "He threatened her. He was in the garden when the crime was committed——"

She raised her hand, as if to ward off a blow.

"In the garden?" she shivered. "He was in the garden ... then?"

"He will require much assistance," continued the huge unknown—"and there is no time to lose. Will you help him?"

"I would die for him," she choked. "What can I do?"

The stranger re-opened the door.

"Come with me, mademoiselle," he said softly—"and I will tell you."

Chapter XVI

A Triple Alliance

He led the girl out of the house. At the corner of the street a taxi was waiting. He opened the door.

"Where are we going?" she demanded suspiciously.

"To the Hotel Savoy, mademoiselle," he answered.

She hung back.

"Why should I go with you?" she asked defiantly. "I have never seen you before. I don't know who you are."

"Mademoiselle," he replied, "your friend is in great danger. He will not be able to help himself. If you do not come with me, you will not be able to help him. And I assure you that he needs your help."

She got in without another word. He placed himself beside her, and the car started.

"Who are you?" she asked.

"My name," he told her, "is Dupont—Victorien Dupont. I arrived in London from Paris a few days ago."

"What have you to do with this?" she said doubtfully.

"That," he replied, "I cannot at the moment explain to you. I am concerned in this case for reasons of my own, which must remain my own for the present. I was in the garden when Christine Manderson was killed."

She started, staring at him.

"You were in the garden too?" she cried.

"I was," he affirmed. "And I know that Monsieur Layton did not kill her."

"He didn't!" she declared. "He couldn't kill anything. He spends his time giving life—not taking it."

"The police will be satisfied that he did, and they will have a strong case. Unless we can help him by discovering the truth in time, he will not be able to clear himself. Are you prepared to work for him?"

"I told you," she repeated passionately, "I would die for him."

"It is well," he said. "There will be three people on his side. You—my friend, Mr. Tranter, who was also in the garden—and myself. Together we will save him. There will be separate tasks for us all. Mr. Tranter will be waiting at the hotel when we arrive, and we will settle our plan of campaign. Until then, mademoiselle, let us not refer to the subject again. Do me the favor thoroughly to compose yourself. In these matters coolness is of the utmost importance."

He compressed himself further into his corner, and closed his eyes. The girl said nothing more. The rapidity of the whole catastrophe, and the sudden appearance of this new adventure bewildered her. The huge mysterious stranger almost frightened her. Though his eyes were shut and he made neither sound nor movement, she felt that he was searching her, that he was straining all his mental forces to steal the thoughts that were throbbing through her mind. As they drew near to their destination, she fiercely exerted the self-control that was one of her least developed virtues, and by the time they reached the Savoy, and Monsieur Dupont opened his eyes, she was steady and watchful.

"Mademoiselle," said Monsieur Dupont softly, "you will be of the greatest assistance. Already you know the value of silence."

In his private sitting-room they found Tranter awaiting them.

"My friend," said Monsieur Dupont, "this lady will work with us. She is much attached to James Layton, and her assistance will be most valuable." He turned to her. "Mademoiselle, I have not the honor...."

"My name's Jenny West," she said, comprehending the request.

"Where is Layton?" Tranter asked, as Monsieur Dupont placed a chair for the girl, and sat down himself.

"By this time," Monsieur Dupont replied, "he will have arrived at Scotland Yard. Our friend Inspector Fay will question him, and he will certainly be detained. As I have just explained to mademoiselle, he is in great danger. Unless we succeed in our object, his position is without hope."

Tears welled up in the girl's eyes, but she checked them with an effort.

"I wish," Monsieur Dupont continued, with careful emphasis, "that my own position also should be clearly understood, in so far as I am at liberty to explain it. I cannot yet tell you how I come to be interested in this affair. Soon I may do so—but until then you must be content to take me on trust, and to accept my assurance that I am fully qualified to direct you. Are you willing to follow my instructions without question—to save this innocent man, who will be accused of a horrible crime which he did not commit?"

"Yes, yes," the girl cried. "I am ready. I will do anything."

"And I," said Tranter.

"The directions I give may seem to be strange," Monsieur Dupont went on impressively—"but they must be followed. The errands on which I send you may seem to be unimportant and even foolish—but they must be carried out. Do not look for explanations, until I make them. I give account to no one. Those who work with me work much in the dark—but they reach the light. There must be no hesitation. Is that understood?"

Again the others agreed.

"Then," said Monsieur Dupont confidently, "we shall succeed. Layton will be saved—but it will be a hard and difficult task. The first law I have to impose on you is—silence. Complete silence, to every one except myself."

He turned to the girl.

"At three o'clock this afternoon, mademoiselle, unless you hear from me to the contrary, you will go to Scotland Yard, where Mr. Layton will be detained. That I shall verify by telephone. You will see him, and you will tell him this: You will say that I, Dupont, know how and why Christine Manderson died—that I, and those with me, will not allow the innocent to suffer—and that he shall be delivered from this charge. And say to him, also, anything from yourself that you may wish to say."

They were both gazing at him blankly.

"You know?" the girl gasped. "You know who killed her?"

The great Frenchman seemed to develop before their eyes into a figure of tremendous menace, every inch of him alive with implacable, relentless purpose.

"I know," he declared slowly, "just what I have told you—how and why she died. Ask me no more. Remember our conditions. There must be no questions until the time comes."

He rose, and took an envelope from his pocket.

"Certain things that I shall ask you to do, mademoiselle, may involve expense. In this envelope you will find a sufficient sum. Do not hesitate to accept it. Ample funds are at our command. When you return from Scotland Yard, report to me here. If I am not in, wait for me. And, above all, remember—silence."

He opened the door, and bowed her out. Then he turned to Tranter with a faint smile.

"Well, my friend?" he asked quietly.

"Do you really mean," Tranter exclaimed, "that you know the truth of the crime?"

Monsieur Dupont offered him a cigar, and lit one himself with great composure.

"I know just as much about the crime, my friend, as I have said. I repeat—I know how and why that unfortunate woman died. Who, or what, caused her to die is another matter, which we are setting ourselves to solve."

"You are certain that Layton is innocent?"

"James Layton did not commit the crime," Monsieur Dupont returned firmly. "But he will be hanged for it—if we are not in time."

"Well," said Tranter, "what is there for me to do?"

"For you," replied Monsieur Dupont, "there is the most important task in the case, so far. And the most dangerous. Within twenty-four hours you must discover, and bring to me here, the secret of the Crooked House."

"Good Lord!" Tranter exclaimed, taken aback, "how on earth am I to do that?"

"I do not know," Monsieur Dupont admitted. "Nor have I any helpful suggestions to make. The method of procedure I leave to you."

"Housebreaking is entirely out of my province," Tranter objected. "And the secret of that house, if there is one, is likely to be very well guarded."

"Probably," agreed Monsieur Dupont. "But the fact remains that before the end of the next twenty-four hours I must have that secret—and you are the person who must bring it to me."

Tranter took up his hat and stick, without further protest.

"Very well," he said stoutly. "I will do my best."

Monsieur Dupont looked at his watch.

"It is one o'clock," he said, opening the door. "At one o'clock to-morrow I shall be waiting for you in this room."

Chapter XVII

Mr. Gluckstein In Confidence

Mrs. Astley-Rolfe invariably received her creditors in pink deshabille.

The financier, Mr. Solomon Gluckstein, original and senior representative of John Brown & Co., Jermyn Street, was particularly fond of pink, and extremely susceptible to deshabille. Whiskey-and-soda, personally prepared for him in sufficient strength by his charming debtor, increased the fondness and the susceptibility.

"Ma tear lady," said Mr. Gluckstein, with desperate firmness, "I have come on an unplethant errand."

Mrs. Astley-Rolfe pouted petulantly.

"Am I to have no peace?" she complained, from an alluring attitude on a couch. "Isn't it enough to have gone through the last two days? Look at me. I am a nervous wreck."

"Then all women wouldth with to be nervouth wrecks," said Mr. Gluckstein gallantly.

"I believe that odious detective actually imagined at the beginning that I might have murdered the poor girl."

"Nonthenth," the financier assured her.

"I have scarcely had any sleep," she went on reproachfully. "It is a wonder I am not thoroughly ill. And now you—from whom I should have expected consideration—come here with a face like a rock, and announce your intention to be unpleasant. If I didn't know you so well, I might have believed you."

Mr. Gluckstein glanced towards the door, and drew his chair closer to her.

"Let us understand each other," he said deliberately. "At the present time you owe me a large thum of money."

"Gospel truth," she admitted.

"Very much more than you could pothibly pay, if I came down on you."

She uttered a sigh of relief.

"At last you realize that!" she exclaimed thankfully.

"Also," continued Mr. Gluckstein, "you owe money to various other people."

"Your veracity," she confessed, "is beyond question."

"Almosth ath much ath you owe to me."

"Quite as much," she said cheerfully.

59

"And you owe me," he continued—"twelve thousand poundth."

"The first time I have looked the evil fully in the face," she shuddered.

His small eyes regarded her intently.

"The last half of that—I lent to you on a certain understanding."

"Understanding?" she echoed languidly.

"Yeth."

"What did you understand?"

"That you intended to become engaged to George Copplesthone, who would pay your debths when you married him."

A quick change swept over her. She became hard and calculating.

"Well?" she returned.

"You have not become engaged to him."

"No."

"Some one elth became engaged to him."

"Yes," she said calmly.

"That doth not look," he concluded, "like fulfillment of the understanding."

"Doesn't it?" she retorted.

He glanced again at the door, and came still closer.

"Lithen," he said slowly. "I have been your friendth. I have done for you what I would not have done for any one elth. I have treated you fairly, and I have never prethed you."

She softened immediately.

"You have been very kind to me," she said gratefully.

"You muth be my friendth too. I muth tell you my thecret. Promith me faithfully that you will keep it."

She looked at him in astonishment.

"Certainly I will keep it," she agreed.

"Five days ago," Mr. Gluckstein informed her painfully, "my partner abthconded, and left me almosth a ruined man."

Her face expressed genuine sympathy.

"I am very sorry," she said feelingly. "What a dreadful blow for you."

"It ith unnethecessary to explain bithness details to you," the financier proceeded. "My working capital hath gone, and the fact thimply is that I cannot carry on—unleth——" he paused to give his words additional emphasis, "unleth you repay me my twelve thousand poundth in full within two months."

"Two months?" she exclaimed blankly.

"Two months," he repeatedly firmly. "That ith the utmost time I can give you. Have you any other means of raithing the money?"

"Not a ghost of one," she replied frankly. "I might as well try to push over the Marble Arch as raise a single thousand."

"Then," he said steadily, "if you do not marry Copplesthone I am a bankrupt—and a bankrupt I will not be."

"I shall marry him," she said. "I told you I should—and I shall. You will have your money."

"I believed you," he returned. "But another woman beat you."

She looked away from him.

"Did she?" she replied evenly.

There was silence for a moment.

"When Copplesthone announthed his engagement to Mith Manderthon," the financier went on, "I stood ruined. I admit it. I stood ruined by your defeat. That ith the thecret that you muth keep. I was sure that you had no other means of paying me back. Nothing could save me but a miraculouth removal of the obstacle."

"The obstacle was removed," she said, in the same even tone.

He shuddered.

"It wath. The obstacle that stood between you and Copplesthone, and me and ruination, wath removed. It was a ghastly thing, and we are very thorry. But let uth be candid. It wath to our advantage."

"Yes," she agreed slowly—"it was to our advantage."

"There must not be another obstacle," he said.

"There will not be another," she replied. "George Copplestone will marry me—and you shall have your twelve thousand pounds, as I promised. You need not be anxious."

He looked round the luxurious room, and sighed deeply. It surprised her that she had not noticed before how much he had aged.

"I must begin again," he said. "I am getting old—but I will rebuild my fortune. I will not be the only poor Jew in London."

"You have been a good friend to me," she said gently. "I am very sorry."

He paused to finish his drink, but his crafty eyes never left her face. She did not meet them.

"I wonder," he said, in a slightly lower tone, replacing his empty glass on the table, "what the police will discover."

"I should imagine that there is very little to be discovered," she returned. "There seems no doubt that it was James Layton, the Mad Millionaire, as he is called. He will probably be arrested within the next twenty-four hours. It appears to be a clear case. He threatened her—in front of us all. And he was in the garden."

"It ought to be enough," he admitted, more easily. "What more could they want?"

"The evidence is very strong," she said, lazily settling her deshabille. "Many people have been hanged on less. Apparently the police are satisfied. At least, they have not arrested either of us."

The financier started violently.

"Either of uth?" he cried, aghast. "What do you mean, either of uth?"

Her smile was enigmatical.

"As you said just now—the removal of the obstacle was to the advantage of both of us."

"But they don't know," he shivered. "They can't know."

"I hope not," she said shortly.

Perspiration began to stand out on his forehead. He had lost color considerably.

"You promised to keep my thecret," he exclaimed nervously. "Noth a word to any one."

"I shall keep my promise," she replied.

"There is no cause for alarm. I don't think Inspector Fay will trouble us."

There was a tap at the door. They turned as the butler entered.

"Inspector Fay would like to see you for a few minutes, madam."

They looked at each other. The financier was agitated. The woman was perfectly calm.

"Talk of the devil!" she smiled.

Mr. Gluckstein gripped his hat, stick, and gloves, and rose hurriedly.

"He must not see me here," he said jerkily. "Let me out another way."

"Go through there," she said, pointing to a door at the opposite end of the room, "and when he has come in, Parker will let you out. Bring the inspector in, Parker."

The financier did not wait to shake hands.

"Remember," he whispered passing her—"both your promises."

"They will be kept," she said.

Chapter XVIII

The Wit of the Pink Lady

Inspector Fay entered the room at one end a few seconds after Mr. Gluckstein left it at the other.

Mrs. Astley-Rolfe greeted him in a friendly fashion. She showed considerable strain—but, otherwise, was looking her best. And her best was delightful.

"Good morning, inspector," she said languidly.

"Good morning, madam." He glanced back to make certain that the door was closed. "I trust you have recovered from the shock of the crime."

"I still feel it very much," she replied, shuddering. "It was the most horrible experience I have ever had. To think of seeing that poor girl alive and well one minute, and the next—like that. It's too dreadful to think of."

"It was certainly a most disgusting crime," the inspector agreed.

"I suppose it was James Layton?"

"I am afraid I cannot make any statement at present," he replied. "Our investigations are proceeding as quickly as possible. I hope we shall clear it up in a few days."

"I hope you will," she declared fervently. "Such a brutal criminal can expect no mercy."

"In the meantime," continued the inspector, "I should be much obliged if you would kindly give me a little information."

"Certainly," she said readily. "Sit down."

He sat down, facing her. She made a charming picture. But Inspector Fay had been taken in by charming women several times during the early part of his career, and at this stage of it was as impervious as an oyster.

"Please understand," he began, "that in asking these questions I am making no insinuations or suggestions of any kind. It is necessary to establish certain facts."

"I quite understand," she assured him. "What do you want to know?"

"I want to know what you were saying to Mr. Copplestone in the garden, before Mr. Tranter came to tell him that Miss Manderson had gone into the house."

She started.

"I?" she exclaimed. "I was not with Mr. Copplestone."

He remained silent.

"I told you, I was not with any one. I did not feel quite myself, and strolled about alone."

The inspector's face was quite impassive.

"You wish me to accept that answer?" he asked quietly.

She stiffened haughtily.

"What do you mean?" she said sharply.

"I mean that you wish that answer to be accepted as the truth?"

"Of course. Are you suggesting that it is not?"

"I am suggesting nothing," he returned, with unruffled composure. "But I must tell you that if I am to accept that answer, it may have serious consequences."

"Serious consequences?" she echoed, startled.

"Yes."

"For whom?"

"Possibly for Mr. Copplestone himself."

Signs of uneasiness began to appear, in spite of her wonderful self-control.

"For Mr. Copplestone...?"

"For Mr. Copplestone," the inspector affirmed steadily.

"I don't understand," she said. "Will you kindly explain?"

"Certainly." His voice dropped slightly. "Mr. Copplestone lied to me."

"Lied to you?"

"Lied to me," he repeated. "In accounting for himself, from the time he came out into the garden after dinner until Mr. Tranter found him to deliver Miss Manderson's message, he lied to me deliberately. I want to know why."

"You had better ask him," she retorted. "I do not know."

"Mr. Bolsover, the theatrical manager, told me that he found James Layton lurking by the house, and called to Mr. Copplestone before following him. Mr. Copplestone stated that the reason he did not hear that call was that he had gone into the house to refill his cigarette-case, and did not come out again until just before Mr. Tranter found him after leaving Miss Manderson. That statement was false."

"How do you know?" she asked quickly.

"He did not go into the house to refill his cigarette-case. He had had no opportunity to smoke afterwards, and when I questioned him his case was almost empty. He may have gone in for another reason——or he may not have gone in at all."

"Is it not very trivial?" she said.

"If you had been dealing with crimes and criminals as long as I have," the inspector returned, "you would know that nothing is trivial. At present, Mr. Copplestone's time while the crime was being committed is unaccounted for—and he is detected in a lie. It is not a pleasant position to be in."

She was silent. Her hands moved nervously.

"What is the use of telling me this?" she asked.

"It occurred to me," he replied, "that you might be able to extricate him from that position."

"Why?" she demanded resentfully.

He shrugged his shoulders.

"Can you?" he insisted, watching her closely.

For a moment she paused. There was malevolence in her gaze.

"I do not know what he was doing," she said obstinately.

"Madam," said the inspector impressively, "if George Copplestone stood in the dock in front of you, and his life depended on the truth of your answer—would it still be the same answer?"

She turned on him.

"In the dock? What do you mean?"

"Would it still be the same answer?" he repeated sternly.

"Do you suggest that he may have committed the crime?" she exclaimed contemptuously. "Its absurd!"

"I told you," he said, "I suggest nothing. My case must be complete. I want to know the truth."

Silence followed. She plucked angrily at the lace edge of her gown. Inspector Fay waited imperturbably.

"He was with me," she said, at last, sullenly.

"Thank you," said the inspector.

There was another pause.

"Please go on," he pressed her.

She did not attempt to conceal her resentment at his insistence. But the inspector's attitude was compelling.

"We had a private conversation," she said viciously. "What passed between us concerned only ourselves."

"I have no wish to pry into that," he told her. "But I should like to know why both you and Mr. Copplestone preferred to tell me a falsehood rather than admit that you were talking together in the garden."

"We had our reasons," she snapped, "for not wishing it to be known that we had been together. We had no time to speak privately after the crime was discovered, and it evidently seemed best to both of us, rather than risk conflicting statements, not to admit that we had spoken to each other at all. I hope you have nothing more to ask me."

The inspector rose.

"I have nothing more to ask you, madam," he said politely. "I trust it will not be necessary for me to trouble you again in this case. But if it should be—you will find that in such serious matters it is always better to speak the truth. Good morning."

He walked quickly out of the room, leaving a lady in pink deshabille quivering with an emotion that was not anger, but a new triumph.

Chapter XIX

Detained on Suspicion

Inspector Fay left the house of the lady in pink with a satisfied expression on his face. At the corner of the street he hailed a taxi, and drove to Scotland Yard.

Under the watchful eyes of his escort, James Layton awaited him. The millionaire was perfectly composed, and appeared to be under no apprehension as to the outcome of his visit. He accompanied the inspector to a private room, and sat down in a comfortable chair without the smallest sign of alarm.

"Mr. James Layton?" the inspector began, seating himself at a table.

"Yes."

"Mr. Layton, I am Inspector Fay—in charge of the investigations of the death of Miss Christine Manderson, at Richmond, on Tuesday night. I want you to be good enough to answer the questions I have to ask you as clearly as possible."

"Certainly," the young man replied, unhesitatingly.

"To begin with—did you go to Richmond on that night?"

"I did."

"Were you alone?"

"I was."

"Did you call at Mr. Copplestone's house at half-past eight?"

"Yes."

"You asked to see Mr. Copplestone?"

"Yes."

"And he refused to see you?"

"He did."

"What was your object in calling on him, in that manner, at such an inconvenient time?"

"I had just ascertained that Miss Manderson had, or was about to, become engaged to marry him. My object was to tell him that he was not a fit person to be her husband, and that I would prevent the marriage at all costs."

"That you would prevent the marriage?"

"Yes."

"Because, in your opinion, he was unworthy of her?"

"Totally."

"Had you any right to take upon yourself the control of Miss Manderson's choice of a husband?"

"No right, perhaps—as you use the term."

"As any one would use it?"

"To my mind, yes."

"To your mind you had a right to interfere in that engagement?"

"Yes."

"We will come back to that presently," the inspector proceeded. "What did you do when Mr. Copplestone refused to see you?"

"I am afraid my excitement got the better of me. I forced my way past the servant, and went into a room from which I heard voices, thinking that he was there with her."

"You knew, then, that she was in the house at the time?"

"Yes. I had previously telephoned to her hotel, and her maid had told me that she was spending the evening at Copplestone's house."

"I am told you burst into the room uttering her name."

"Possibly."

"But you found only some guests of Mr. Copplestone's, who had been invited to dinner?"

"Yes."

"Was there anything strange about the room?"

"It was decorated in an extraordinary manner."

"I think you made some remark about the decorations?"

"Perhaps I did. I had been told something of Mr. Copplestone's eccentricities, and I inferred that the engagement was an accomplished fact, and that the decorations had been put up in celebration of it."

"Do you remember saying anything else in the room?"

"I said that rather than allow Miss Manderson to be engaged to George Copplestone, I would tear her to pieces with my own hands."

"And utterly destroy her?"

"Yes."

"A somewhat violent announcement," the inspector observed.

"I am afraid it was."

"You were in a state of great excitement, were you not?"

"I was very excited."

"Almost beside yourself?"

"I cannot say that."

"Were you responsible for your words and actions at the time?"

"Perfectly."

"You really meant what you said?"

"I meant what I said," the young man declared calmly.

The inspector was writing rapidly.

"You were then requested to leave the house, and I think you left quite quietly?"

68

"Yes."

"What did you do then?"

"I climbed over the wall into the garden and waited for an opportunity to get into the house again and speak to Copplestone or Miss Manderson."

"You were behaving rather strangely, were you not, Mr. Layton?" the inspector asked.

"I suppose I was."

"If you had heard of any one else acting in the same way, you would have thought that he could hardly have been in a normal state of mind?"

"I expect I should."

"Yet you say you were quite yourself?"

"I was quite myself."

"And prepared to carry out your threat?"

"I do not know what I was prepared to do. I did not carry it out."

"Later on, one of the guests, Mr. Bolsover, found you creeping round the house towards an open window?"

"Yes."

"Before he ran after you, do you remember hearing him call to Mr. Copplestone?"

"Yes, he did."

"Was there any answer?"

"I did not hear one."

"Mr. Bolsover then followed you out in the direction in which the crime was committed?"

"I do not know where the crime was committed," Layton replied firmly. "I know nothing of the crime."

"Whoever committed it managed to fulfill your own threat fairly fully."

"Unfortunately, yes."

"Have you any suggestion to make as to who that person may have been?"

"No."

"What, then, did you do when Mr. Bolsover ran after you?"

"I eluded him in the darkness, climbed over the wall again, and went away."

"Without having fulfilled your object?"

"Yes."

"Had you seen anything at all of Miss Manderson, or Mr. Copplestone?"

"Nothing."

There was a pause. James Layton waited quietly while the

inspector finished off his notes. His face was a trifle paler than before, but he betrayed no sign of agitation.

"Now," resumed the inspector, "let us go back. You said that to your mind you had a right to interfere in Miss Manderson's engagement?"

"I did."

"What had given you that right?"

"I am sorry," the young man returned courteously—"but I decline to answer that question."

"When and where did you first meet her?"

"I cannot tell you."

"You would be wiser to do so."

"Possibly."

The inspector's face darkened.

"Mr. Layton," he said, with unmistakable emphasis, "you had better not decline to answer any question. I must warn you that your position may become extremely serious."

"I am afraid," Layton remarked quietly, "that you have already made up your mind that I am guilty of the crime."

"That is as it may be," replied the inspector. "I am advising you for your own good. To refuse to answer questions is not the way to allay suspicion—but to increase it."

"I realize that," the young man said. "But I still refuse."

Inspector Fay leant back in his chair patiently.

"Come, Mr. Layton, you will only put us to the trouble and delay of proving what you might as well tell us at once. And it will do you no good."

"I should be sorry to cause you any additional trouble," Layton replied. "But I have my reasons."

"Let me help you," continued the inspector. "I have had inquiries made at Miss Manderson's hotel, at the theater at which she was to have appeared, of her maid, and various other sources. We have got her time pretty well accounted for. It seems that you have not seen her at all since she arrived in this country two months ago. Is that so?"

There was no answer.

"Anyway, if you did see her once or twice, there were certainly no opportunities for anything to develop between you to account for your behavior, or justify to the right to which you considered yourself entitled. You must have known her before."

Layton was still silent. The inspector continued easily.

"I am wondering whether a cable across the Atlantic would bring me a description of a certain Michael Cranbourne, once well known in the United States—particularly in Chicago—son of a multi-millionaire."

James Layton stiffened in his chair. He had become white and tense.

"A large part in the career of Michael Cranbourne was played by an adventuress named Thea Colville—said, at one time, to have been the most beautiful woman in America—and known later, on the stage in New York, as Christine Manderson."

The young man rose. On his face there was a wonderful new dignity and calm—a relief, as if some heavy burden had dropped from him and left him free.

"Yes," he said quietly, "I am Michael Cranbourne. I might have admitted it at first. What do you want now?"

"The whole story," the inspector replied, motioning him back to his chair.

"I will tell you," he said.

He sat down again. A great contentment seemed to rest upon him, as on one who reaches the end of a difficult and tiring journey. There was a long pause.

"I first met Thea Colville," he began, at last, "in Chicago, when I was twenty-five—seven years ago. She was twenty. It would be no use attempting to give you an idea of what she was like. You never saw her alive. No description could convey an impression of her beauty—of her awful fascination. From the moment I first saw her there was no other woman in my world. I was engaged to be married, but I put an end to it. People said I behaved badly, but I didn't care. I couldn't look at, or think of, another woman after I had seen her. She enslaved me. I was hers, body and soul. She held me helpless. I was only one of many, but I was a favored one—at least, I thought so."

He told his story slowly, in a low voice, without emotion. He was staring out straight in front of him, forgetful of his surroundings and his listener. The past held him.

"My family warned me, and threatened me. I knew they were telling me the truth—but I wouldn't listen. I hadn't been brought up to care what results my actions brought on other people. I thought only of myself—of the indulgence of my own desires. I lived a useless, contemptible life—entirely without scruples or restraints. There was scarcely a vice that I was not steeped in—hardly a sin that I had not explored. I had enough money to gratify all my senses. Nothing was beneath me. I plunged into every depravity. I made new depths for myself." He clenched his hands. "And I led others after me."

71

There was another pause. He sat rigid. The inspector waited patiently.

"I need not trouble you with unnecessary details," the low voice went on. "It is enough that for her sake I sacrificed all my prospects—I threw away my heritage. To keep her for myself I squandered every cent I could lay my hands on. I robbed my own brother. I forged my father's name. I did ... other things. It was only the generosity of my family that kept me from gaol. And Thea threw me over."

"Apparently," the inspector remarked, not unsympathetically, "her standard of morality was on a somewhat similar level."

"She is dead," said the young man gently. "'De mortuis nil nisi bonum.'"

The inspector shrugged his shoulders.

"As you please," he said. "Go on."

"She refused to see me—to have anything more to do with me. She cut me out of her life with one stroke. For the first time I knew she hadn't cared. That broke me. I was very ill. For a year I knew no one. I couldn't hear or speak. They fed me like a child. They thought I was mad"—his eyes began to gleam unnaturally, his words quickened—"but in reality I was in the presence of God. I was in the image I had brought upon my soul—black, hideous, distorted, reeking with the filth of my sins. I saw myself—in all the degradation I had brought upon the Shape of God. I saw my own page in the Book of Life. All the entries were on the debit side. The credit side was bare. I waited for damnation—but there is no damnation. There is only Building. I went out from the presence of God—a Builder."

His face was transformed. His voice rang with triumph—with the pride of victory.

"I came to myself. It was like waking from the dead. It was a long time before I recovered even a little of my strength. Every hand was against me—except my mother's. She stood by me. When she died, a year later, I inherited the whole of her fortune. The others tried to take it away from me, but I fought them. I had new uses for the money. I came over to this country, and began my work. For four years I have given myself and all I have. Go and see for yourself what I have done. Go and see the men, women, and children who would die for me. Go and hear them bless my name. Hear of the lives I have built—the light I have brought. I have filled up my credit side. I have a balance in hand in the Book of Life."

Inspector Fay remained silent. He was a severely practical man. Before his mind there was only the outcome of the interview. The young man controlled himself with an effort. His excitement passed. He was again quiet and composed.

"None of my old passions or inclinations remained—except my love for Thea. I couldn't crush it. I fought against it with all my strength. I struggled to stamp it out, but it was unconquerable. Her face was always in front of me, day and night. Her voice was always in my ears. I couldn't escape. I heard nothing more of her until about six weeks ago, when I saw a photograph of her in one of the papers under the name of Christine Manderson, with a statement that she had arrived in London to play at the Imperial Theater. The longing to see her again was too strong for me. Day after day I waited outside the stage-door of the theater—until she came, in all her fatal, maddening beauty. We stood facing each other ... and she passed me by without a word."

His voice broke. He pressed his thin hands together.

"The madness came over me again. The sight of her fanned all the old flames. I was on fire. I tried to follow her, but they kept me out. I wrote to her that night, telling her what I had done, how I had suffered, and begging, imploring her to let me see her. The answer was a curt note, in the third person, saying that she declined to receive any communication from me whatsoever."

Again he paused. The inspector made no comment.

"I found out where she was staying, what her plans were, and who were her friends. I discovered that she had come under the influence of George Copplestone, who is little better than I was once. The thought that she was to be the sport of his depravity drove me to frenzy. I neglected my work. I could do nothing. Then I heard that they were on the point of becoming engaged. The rest you know. I followed her to Copplestone's house. She had evidently warned him against me. I forced my way into the room, calling her by the name of Christine——"

"Why?" the inspector asked

"Because it was obvious that she would not wish the name of Thea Colville to be known to London. That is all I have to tell you."

The inspector rose.

"Mr. Cranbourne," he said formally, "after hearing your story, I am afraid I have no option but to detain you on suspicion of having caused the death of Christine Manderson, otherwise Thea Colville, and to warn you that anything you say may be used in evidence against you."

The young man heard him without a tremor.

"I did not kill her," he said firmly. "God's will be done."

Chapter XX

The Birth of the Killer

Monsieur Dupont was one of those fortunate individuals who can sleep in a train.

He left Paddington at one o'clock, and slept for an hour, a sleep of childlike ease and innocence. When he woke the train was within five minutes of his destination. He alighted at a small country station, and instituted inquiries for a conveyance.

Twenty minutes later, an unimpressionable horse, attached to a hybrid vehicle, was jogging him along country lanes which would have delighted a man with less serious purposes. But Monsieur Dupont was too much occupied with the uglinesses of humanity to heed the beauties of nature. It was not until they arrived at the outskirts of a small village that he began to look about him with interest.

It was a lovely spot, nestling in primeval innocence under the shelter of protecting hills. Monsieur Dupont uttered a heavy sigh, and spoke, for the first time during the drive, to the stout, sunburnt lad who conducted the equipage.

"My friend," he said sorrowfully, "who could imagine that such a corner of heaven could have been the cradle of one of the most terrible tragedies of the world? I feel like a purveyor of sins, creeping into the preserves of God."

The startled stare that confronted him was not helpful to further conversation. The disconcerted youth vigorously obtained fresh impetus from their source of progress, and drew up at length, with obvious relief, before a low, creeper-covered house, lying in a nest of flowers.

Monsieur Dupont's gentle knock produced a rubicund housekeeper, of about eighty, who blended in perfect harmony with the house, the creeper, and the flowers.

"Doctor Lessing, if you please, madame," said Monsieur Dupont.

He was shown into a small library, opening on to the garden. The room was flooded with sunshine. There were flowers everywhere.

"Mon Dieu," said Monsieur Dupont, aloud, "that I should come to ask such questions here."

He turned as the door opened, and bowed before a sturdy, white-haired old man, bronzed with the health of the country.

"Monsieur Dupont?" said the doctor. "What can I do for you?"

Monsieur Dupont took a letter from his pocket, and unfolded it.

"Monsieur, I beg you to read this letter. It is from the French Embassy, and begs assistance to me in an investigation that I am making."

Doctor Lessing read the letter, and returned it.

"I shall be happy to assist you in any way I can," he said, courteously. "Please sit down."

Monsieur Dupont sat down by the open windows and drank in the fragrance of the garden.

"Doctor Lessing," he began, "I believe it is for a long time that you have lived in this beautiful place?"

"For forty-five years," the old doctor smiled contentedly. "But I am by no means one of its oldest inhabitants. Lives are long in the country. To what period do you wish to refer?"

"A period," Monsieur Dupont replied, "nearly forty years ago. I do not know exactly."

"A long stretch," said Doctor Lessing ruefully. "But my memory shall do its best for you. That is all I can promise."

"I am engaged," said Monsieur Dupont, "on an extraordinary quest. I do not think that any human being has ever been engaged on a more extraordinary quest."

"A pleasant one, I trust," said the doctor.

"As much to the contrary as it is possible to imagine."

The doctor murmured a regret and waited for his huge visitor to continue.

"Do you," Monsieur Dupont inquired, "recollect the name of Winslowe?"

Doctor Lessing started slightly.

"Winslowe?"

"Oscar Winslowe."

A keen glance flashed from the doctor's eyes.

"Yes," he said quickly, "I recollect the name."

"He lived, I think in this village at the time I have said?"

"Yes." The reply was a trifle curt.

"Perhaps," Monsieur Dupont proceeded evenly, "there were circumstances in connection with that name which helped to fix it in your memory?"

"There were certain circumstances," the doctor admitted, "which made it a name that I am unlikely to forget."

"Unpleasant circumstances?" queried Monsieur Dupont.

"The most unpleasant that have ever occurred to me in the whole length of my practice."

"It is for that story," said Monsieur Dupont, "that I have come to ask. May I beg all the details that you can recall?"

"Perhaps you will first tell me," the doctor returned, "for what purpose you require this information?"

"I require it," Monsieur Dupont replied impressively, "to save the life of an innocent man, who is wrongly accused of the crime of murder. I require it also prove three deaths, and possibly to prevent another three."

Again the doctor started. His hands gripped the arms of his chair.

"Three deaths?" he exclaimed sharply. "What do you mean?"

"Three deaths," repeated Monsieur Dupont. "Of three very beautiful women."

The doctor sprang to his feet.

"My God!" he cried hoarsely.

"Will you tell me the story?" said Monsieur Dupont.

Doctor Lessing sat down again in his chair. He was considerably shaken. He leant back and closed his eyes, remaining silent for a few moments.

"I think," he began at last, "that I can, at all events, remember the chief facts of the case. It was such a remarkable and distressing one that it stands out in the annals of such a peaceful spot as this, and it has therefore remained in my memory, though so much else has faded. But you must make allowances for the flight of time. Look out of the window to the left, and you will see a large red house, on the slope of the hill."

"I see it," said Monsieur Dupont, following the direction.

"That was Oscar Winslowe's house, forty years ago. Winslowe was an unprincipled and dissolute man. He was only about twenty-five or six at that time, but already he was sodden with drink, drugs, and vice of every description. He was the worst kind of blackguard. But his wife was the exact opposite to him, a gentle, delicate girl. She was not beautiful, but her nature more than compensated for lack of beauty. He had married her for her money, and treated her abominably. I became friendly with her, partly because of the pity I felt for her on account of his treatment, and partly because I sincerely admired the beauty of her character. In consequence of that friendship, I undertook to watch over her entry into motherhood."

"That is what I want," said Monsieur Dupont. "Her entry into motherhood."

"The more I saw of her," continued the doctor, "the greater grew my pity. There have been wonderful women in the world who have made history by their patience and endurance—but this woman was one of those, equally brave and equally patient, of whom history knows nothing. She worshipped her husband, blindly, dumbly—as an animal will still love the man or woman who ill-treats it. She never uttered a word of complaint or blame. Her greatest hope was that the advent of the child would induce from him something of the consideration and tenderness that he had never given her. She believed it was some fault, some shortcoming, of hers that had kept it from her. It didn't occur to her that it might be the beauty of another woman."

"Ah!" said Monsieur Dupont eagerly.

"She discovered that about three months before the child was born. I can't remember how the discovery came about. She followed him to London—and found him, even that short time before the birth of his child, lavishing on a beautiful society woman all that should have been hers."

In spite of the years that had passed the doctor's voice still rose in anger. He paused, checking himself.

"Before that supreme insult, that shattering of her hopes, the poor girl lost her reason. In the state of her health, it was not surprising. She, who would never have harmed a fly, who had never wished ill to any one in her life, became possessed with an awful fury to stamp out the beauty that had robbed her—to destroy the face and body that were more to the man she loved than her own. The other woman, undeserving of consideration as she was, narrowly escaped a horrible punishment. The unfortunate girl was brought back here, and I was sent for to attend her. She grew worse hour after hour. Her mind was completely unhinged. From a furious hatred of the beauty of the woman who had wronged her, the mania increased into a furious hatred of beauty in any shape or form, and a savage lust to destroy it. In the house there were many portraits of the beautiful women of the Winslowe family. She tore the pictures to shreds. There were statues and valuable works of art. She smashed them all to pulp. Her madness was the most terrible thing I have ever seen. She had to be forcibly restrained."

Monsieur Dupont listened intently. There was an expression of triumph on his face.

"A pitiful story," he said softly.

"She partially recovered in a few weeks," the doctor went on, "and before the three months were up her reason, if not actually sound again, was at least restored. But she was a wreck of a woman. There was darkness all round her. She heard nothing more of Winslowe. He never came back to the house. The madness returned when she gave birth to her child, and she died in an asylum a fortnight afterwards."

A longer pause followed. The recitation of his memories moved the good old doctor as the actual experience must have moved the young man of forty years before. He rose, and walked to the window, sniffing the scent of the flowers with relief.

"She left the care of the child to the nurse who was devoted to her, with ample funds for its future. When the affairs were settled up, the nurse took the child away with her, and I have not seen her since."

He made a relieved gesture.

"That is the whole story," he said.

"The nurse," inquired Monsieur Dupont, "what was her name?"

"Masters. Miss Elizabeth Masters."

"Is she still alive?"

"So far as I know she is," the doctor replied. "But I should not have been likely to have heard of her death, if it had taken place."

"Can you assist me to discover her address?"

"She wrote to me periodically," Doctor Lessing returned. "She was an excellent nurse, and I got her some cases in town. But it is a long time since I last heard from her. There may be one or two old letters of hers in my desk. If you will excuse me for a moment, I will see if I can find them for you."

He left the room. Monsieur Dupont turned to the window, and gazed dreamily out into the sunshine.

"And so," he muttered—"in this corner of paradise the Destroyer was born."

Chapter XXI

A Hasty Flight

Doctor Lessing re-entered the room with a letter in his hand.

"The last address I can find," he said, "is 35, De Vere Terrace, Streatham. That is sixteen years old, but as it tells me that she had only just moved in, you might find her still there."

Monsieur Dupont made a note of the address.

"There remains only one question," he said, replacing his pocketbook. "Can you tell me the name of the child?"

The doctor shook his head.

"I'm afraid I can't. The child was christened in the church here, but I was away at the time, and when I returned Miss Masters had gone to London."

"It is very important," said Monsieur Dupont. "Perhaps I can discover it at the church?"

"You will not find any one to tell you at this time," the doctor replied. "But, if you will leave me your address, I will send over to the parsonage this evening and ask Mr. Wickham to turn it up in the register, and let you know."

Monsieur Dupont delivered himself of profuse thanks. Five minutes later he had taken leave of the old doctor, and was returning to the station under the guidance of the sunburnt youth, who was obviously relieved when the expedition terminated.

He slept peacefully until the train reached Paddington.

It was five o'clock when he returned to the Savoy. The girl, Jenny West, was waiting for him. She was as white as death.

"They have charged him," she sobbed. "He is remanded for a week."

He laid a hand gently on her shoulder.

"Do not be afraid," he said. "He will be saved. I have given my word—the word of Dupont—that he will be saved."

He sat down at his writing table, and wrote rapidly for several minutes. He covered four or five sheets of paper, and placed them in an envelope.

"Here, mademoiselle," he said, rising, "are your instructions for to-morrow morning. Do not read them until you are alone. A car will be waiting for you here at ten o'clock in the morning. In the afternoon you will be at liberty to visit Monsieur Layton. I shall expect to see you here at one o'clock."

79

He bowed her out of the room. Half an hour later, he was on his way to Streatham.

A grim expression settled on his face as the journey proceeded, yet it was not altogether unmixed with pity. He was a man of ready sympathy. The doctor's story had evidently moved him to view his task with a new compassion.

As his car turned into De Vere Terrace, he became alert, and scrutinized the houses closely. They were small semi-detached villas. He alighted in front of number 35, passed up the carefully kept front garden, and knocked at the door.

There was no response. He knocked again, several times, but the silence of the house remained undisturbed. He left the door, and glanced in at the front windows, but the room was so dark that he could discern nothing. He walked round to the back. Through the uncurtained kitchen windows he saw a fire in the range. It had almost burnt itself out. There were cooking utensils on the table. Some pastry was rolled out on a board. Apparently the household operations had been somewhat rudely interrupted, and very hastily abandoned. The back door and windows were securely fastened. Returning to the front, he carefully closed the gate, and knocked at the door of the adjoining house.

The name of the house was "Sans Souci," and the door was opened by a lady in rich purple, with a string of pearls.

Monsieur Dupont swept off his hat.

"Madame, I make a thousand apologies! Can you tell me when I shall find Miss Masters at home."

His extreme bulk and the fact that he was not an Englishman seemed to cause the lady considerable amusement.

"I'm sure I don't know," she said engagingly. "I think she's gone away."

"Away?" Monsieur Dupont echoed.

"She left in a great hurry two hours ago," the lady informed him. "In a motor."

Monsieur Dupont appeared somewhat staggered.

"Two hours ago...." he muttered.

"I heard a noise going on in the house," continued the lady, "as if she was packing quickly. She went off with a couple of boxes, and seemed very impatient."

"It is most unfortunate," said Monsieur Dupont mildly. "I have come all the way from the Strand to see her."

The lady laughed freely.

"I'm very sorry," she said good-naturedly. "Won't you come in and rest a bit?"

"Madame," he said, "you are very good, but I must return to the Strand. Would you allow me to ask you some questions, without finding me impertinent?"

"What are they?" she asked.

"Will you tell me if any particular person was in the habit of visiting Miss Masters?"

The lady stiffened slightly.

"Are you a friend of Miss Masters?" she inquired, shortly.

"I am not," Monsieur Dupont admitted frankly. "I have never seen her. It is a few hours ago that I heard her name for the first time."

"I really cannot answer any questions to a stranger," said the lady stiffly. "I don't know you."

Monsieur Dupont bowed.

"If you did, madame," he said, "I should be the proudest of men. Do me the favor to read this letter."

He produced the letter from the French Embassy, and handed it to her. She read it, and was duly impressed.

"Of course I'll do anything for the French Embassy," she said, returning the letter with dignity. "Miss Masters wasn't what you might call a friend of mine. I used to speak to her because she lived in the next house, but it didn't go beyond that. She kept very much to herself. I don't want to say anything at all unkind, but very few ladies in our set knew her. Of course it wasn't her fault, but she was not exactly classy. And when one lives in a neighborhood like this, it's class that tells."

Monsieur Dupont bowed again.

"Obviously, madame," he said.

"The only person that used to visit her," continued the gratified lady, "was a man who often used to arrive in the evening and stay the night. We understood she was an old nurse of his, or something of the kind, and that he more or less provided for her."

"And this man, madame—what was he like?"

"He was rather tall," she said, "and had a dark moustache. He was always well dressed, and looked quite a gentleman."

"You heard his name?"

"No—we never heard his name. I did tell my house-parlor-maid to try to find out once, but she couldn't. Miss Masters actually accused me of prying."

"Mon Dieu," said Monsieur Dupont.

"We had a bit of a row," said the lady candidly.

"Does she live alone, madame?"

"Yes, quite alone. She does everything for herself."

"My last question," said Monsieur Dupont, "may seem remarkable. It is this. Have strange things appeared to be happening in the house during the visits of the tall gentleman with the dark moustache?"

She started, looking at him curiously.

"Strange things?" she repeated slowly.

"Perhaps—violent things."

"Well, that's queer," she exclaimed. "As a matter of fact, we once heard the most extraordinary noises going on when he was there. My husband thought of sending in to ask if anything was the matter."

"What kind of noises, madame?"

"Like as it might be heavy things being thrown about and smashed," said the lady elegantly.

Monsieur Dupont swept off his hat again.

"Thank you, madame," he said—and went back to his car.

Chapter XXII

Tranter Attacks the Crooked House

In the evening, Tranter set off to the Crooked House.

It was dark when he reached it, and the roads were empty. Through the open lodge gates he slipped into the garden unseen. The place seemed deserted. The front of the house showed not a glimmer of light. The whole ugly shape of it stood out gauntly against the sky of the summer night. In the shadow of the trees, he stood watching it, alert to detect a sign of life. But no such sign appeared. The Crooked House was as dark and silent as a tomb.

He crept nearer, keeping under cover of the trees, and skirted the lawns to the back of the house. There, also, darkness reigned. No sound disturbed the stillness. Facing him were the dark shapes of the trees surrounding the wing of the house which extended from the opposite corner. The foliage was so dense that no part of the wing itself was visible. He moved quickly across the back of the house, and reached the trees. As he passed under them, it seemed that he was feeling his way among monstrous sentinels of a dark mystery.

A thick hedge loomed up in front of him. It appeared to surround the entire wing. He walked round, trying to find a place thin enough to allow him to push his way through—but the hedge was evidently there for the express purpose of defeating such an intention. It was impossible to penetrate it, to creep under it, or to climb over it. At the extremity of the wing, about which the trees were thickest, he saw a faint light, escaping round the edge of a blind.

He stopped beneath it. It was a meager, unpleasant light, too dim to be of any greater use in the room than to afford the barest relief from complete darkness. The window was half overgrown with ivy, and he could see that it was filthily dirty. The light continually flickered, and once or twice it seemed to have died out altogether. An eerie sensation began to possess him. He felt very strongly the evil influence of the house. Curiosity to discover what sinister secret it really harbored increased and nerved him.

Again he tried to force a way through the hedge, but everywhere it was an impassable barrier. Slowly and noiselessly he worked his way round the wing, only to find it completely enclosed on all sides. He returned, and stood looking up at the window. Either the light was brighter, or the gap at the edge of the blind had widened. He thought he saw a faint shadow pass and re-pass.

It was not until, in moving to one side, he struck his head against a massive bough of one of the great trees that the possibility of utilizing them as a means of access to the forbidden enclosure occurred to him. He examined the bough. It extended well over the hedge, and would form a perfectly secure bridge. By creeping a few feet along it, he would be able to drop down on the other side of the hedge. Finding the main trunk, he tested his weight on a smaller bough, and swung himself up into the tree.

A few minutes later he stood within the barrier. The window was some twelve or fifteen feet above him. But the walls were thickly clad with ivy, and ivy is an excellent ladder. Carefully he began to climb.

He reached the window, found himself a secure footing, and peered round the edge of the blind. But the light was so poor, and the panes were so dirty, on both sides, that had there been anything to see he could have been very little the wiser. As it was, the small area of the room into which he could dimly peer seemed to be carpetless and unfurnished. There was no movement, no sound. The light itself apparently came from the further end of the room, from the level of a table. He clung on, undecided how to proceed. It appeared that the only thing to do was to wait and listen for some indication of the purpose of the dismal illumination.

He looked at his watch. It was ten-thirty. After a wait of what seemed at least half an hour, he looked again. Ten minutes only had passed. No discernible movement had taken place in the room. Yet he felt perfectly, and very unpleasantly, certain that it was occupied—that something was proceeding within it which, had the blind not intervened, would have revealed the secret of the house. Of what it might be he could form no idea—but, for the first time in his life, he was experiencing, in his mental tenseness and the sinister silence of the surroundings, that sensation which attests a proximity to evil. He was daunted. Fear was a condition to which he was a stranger, but a vivid nervousness was beginning to seize upon him. A sense of personal danger, an element which, so far, he had scarcely considered, was attacking him, and gaining ground. The perspiration was standing out on his face. He found that his hands were cold and wet. The pulses of his body were throbbing; he felt his strength growing less. Muttering a curse, he braced himself with a strong effort. He was accustomed to consider his nerves impregnable. Many times in his life he had known himself to be in far greater danger than he could attribute to the present situation, and such weakness had never assailed him. On four occasions he had been aware that his life was hanging by a thread, and had gloried in his own coolness. And now ... without a doubt the Crooked House was evil.

Still he waited. Another twenty minutes slowly passed.

He started. His hands closed tightly on the trunk of the ivy to which he was clinging. The door of the room had been closed with a slam. He could hear heavy footsteps on the uncarpeted floor. A shadow blotted out the light.

A moment later, a voice—a man's voice, horribly strained and unnatural—rose in a shout of fury.

"Damn you!" it screamed. "Look at your work! Look at it again! Open your rotten eyes and look! Look! Look!"

Tranter was so startled that he almost lost his footing on the ivy. There was no mistaking the voice—it was the scream of madness. He listened for an answer, but there was no sound in response. Then the same voice laughed—a laugh of awful bitterness.

"Are you satisfied? The thing is creeping on. I am getting nearer to you hour by hour. I am more like you to-night. One more grain went yesterday—another to-day. Another will go to-morrow...." Again the voice rose to a shriek of rage and hatred. "Oh, God! There is no hope! No hope! Only on—and on—to that!"

The words trailed off into a sob of agony. Still Tranter could hear no reply.

Silence followed. The shadow again blotted out the light; then sprang aside, and the voice burst out into a fresh paroxysm of madness, yelling a stream of curses at the object of its fury. The madman's frenzy was utterly revolting to listen to, but Tranter searched it closely for some clue to the identity of the person, or thing, to whom it was addressed. The voice rose again to a shriek; then subsided as before into a feeble wail of misery.

"Oh God!" it moaned—"is there no way ... no way? No road but that road? No end but that end? Oh God, have mercy ... have mercy...."

It was a cry of unspeakable anguish—the prayer of a soul in torment. It seemed to Tranter that the speaker had thrown himself down, and was beating the floor with his hands.

There was silence again. Then, for the first time, Tranter became aware of another presence in the room. Though he could neither see nor hear anything, he was conscious of a new, indefinable movement. For a moment horror almost overcame him. He trembled. His nerves failed. The support of the ivy seemed to be giving way under him. He clutched at the framework of the window itself.

The shadow of a figure leapt up from the floor and bounded to the window. The blind was wrenched aside, the window thrown open, and before Tranter had time to recover himself or attempt to escape, the livid, distorted face of George Copplestone was almost touching his own.

A hand closed on his throat in a murderous grip, another seized his wrist. In spite of his frantic struggles, he was dragged with superhuman strength through the window into the room.

Chapter XXIII

A Duel

On the afternoon of the same day, an hour after the departure of Inspector Fay, Mrs. Astley-Rolfe had sped herself to Richmond, in a luxurious motor car, which was her's through the instrumentality of Mr. Gluckstein.

She had found the house of George Copplestone plunged into the darkness of a house of mourning. Every blind was drawn. Every particle of color had been removed or draped. Black reigned supreme.

Copplestone was not pleased to see her, and made no attempt to assume the contrary. He was sitting in his library, moody and melancholy, still in the half-dazed condition into which the death of Christine Manderson had cast him. His face was drawn, haggard, and sickly; his eyes were bloodshot. He looked up at her with a forbidding frown, and did not move from his chair.

"Well?" he said curtly.

She waved a hand round the black room.

"Isn't this ... a trifle theatrical?" she asked coolly.

He said nothing. She sat down opposite to him uninvited. She was perfectly self-possessed.

"Inspector Fay was kind enough to call on me this morning," she remarked pleasantly.

Again there was no reply.

"He may not be an example of dagger-like intelligence," she continued, looking at him steadily—"but he is just a little too sharp to play with."

He scowled at her.

"Have you come to tell me that?" he asked rudely.

"That—and other things," she returned unruffled.

"I don't want to hear them," he retorted.

"They concern you," she said—"rather closely."

"I don't want to hear them," he repeated.

Her lips tightened.

"It is scarcely pleasant to be such an obviously unwelcome visitor," she said evenly. "But I am afraid you must listen."

"I am not in the humor to talk to you," he declared roughly. "I don't want to talk to any one. I want to be left alone. Isn't it enough to be pestered by the police and the papers, and all the damnable business for the inquest? Don't you see that my house is in mourning? Can't you let me be—even for a few days?"

"If I had let you be," she replied easily, "Inspector Fay would probably be here in my place—with much less pleasant intentions."

His glance sharpened.

"What do you mean?" he growled.

"You were not wise," she proceeded tranquilly, "to treat his mental capabilities with quite so much contempt. They are possibly not startlingly brilliant, and he is perfectly easy to deceive. But even an official detective can see through a clumsy lie."

Uneasiness flashed across his face. She smiled slightly.

"And I am afraid, my friend, that you are a clumsy liar."

"I don't know what you are talking about," he snapped.

"Come," she said quietly—"however freely we may trifle with the very much overrated Arm of the Law, at least let us be honest with each other. For some reason or other, you did not tell Inspector Fay the truth."

He sat upright with a jerk, flamed with passion.

"What the devil is it to do with you?" he demanded fiercely.

"I will tell you in a moment," she returned smoothly. "When you accounted for your time to the inspector, you told him that you went into the house to refill your cigarette case?"

His lethargy had disappeared. He leant forward, staring at her, his hands clutching the arms of his chair.

"But, unfortunately, you did not take the elementary precaution of having a full case to support the story. In nine times out of ten you would have got away with it. This was the tenth."

There was silence for a moment. She sat in an easy attitude, meeting his gaze with complete confidence. No trace of his previous dullness remained. He was alert and taut.

She went on, with delightful smoothness.

"With an unpardonable lack of respect for the statement of a gentleman, it occurred to the inspector to test the truth of that account. He did not want to smoke—but he asked you for a cigarette. It was a gentle trap. There were only two in your case."

He ground out an oath under his breath.

"Obviously you had not gone into the house to refill your case. Perhaps you went in for some other reason. Perhaps you didn't go in at all. Anyway, you lied—and when people deliberately lie in such serious cases as these, it may safely be imagined that they have some object to serve in doing so. The inspector was concerned to discover what your object was. So he came to me."

"To you...." he muttered.

"I told you," she returned, "that he is a little too sharp to play with—clumsily. He suspected, from what had been told him, that we might have had a stormy scene together, and had wished to keep it to ourselves. He was quite ready to believe that the time you had failed so lamentably to account for had really been passed with me in 'une petite scène de jalousie.' Fortunately, I had given him a true account of myself, which was that I had been alone. So after the necessary hesitation, and with just the right amount of annoyance, I was able to confess that we had both lied, and that we had in fact been together—and he went away satisfied. I am a better liar than you."

She regarded him serenely. His expression was ugly. There was that in the look of him that might have daunted any woman, but Phyllis Astley-Rolfe had lived chiefly by her wits for a sufficient time to be quite impervious where another would have been silenced. She was as completely without fear as she was without scruple. Her objects were objects to be gained, by the most convenient and speedy means, and quite irrespective of considerations which might have withheld another from attempting to fulfill them. In furtherance of her present object, she gave Copplestone look for look.

"I return good for evil," she said. "It is not a habit of mine. It is really quite contrary to my usual practice. I told a lie to save you from further suspicion. Considering the circumstances, you must admit that it was exceedingly generous of me. And I expect you to be grateful."

Anything but an expression of gratitude confronted her. He remained silent, making a strong effort to mask his agitation. But his fingers twitched spasmodically, and there was unmistakable fear in his eyes. She watched him intently, losing no point of the effect she had created.

"Well...?" she said steadily.

There was no answer. She bent towards him.

"I said you were with me. You were not with me. Where were you?"

The man breathed heavily, his baleful gaze fixed on her. She met it with unassailable composure.

"Listen," she said slowly—"there are strange things in this house. I know it. I've known it for some time. Things that the light of day never shines on. What are they?"

He sprang up, and stood over her with clenched hands, his face torn with fury.

"Damn you!" he cried hoarsely. "What is my house, or what happens in it, to you?"

"Sit down," she said firmly. "You are not frightening me. To threaten a woman is merely to increase her tenacity, and mine requires no fortification. Please move away from me."

He obeyed, muttering. Her calmness disarmed him.

"I am not sure," she continued, "that I wanted you to answer my question—anyway at present. Perhaps your secrets might be too much, even for my conscience—and that is saying a great deal."

He had resumed his chair. There was a moment's pause.

"You were foolish to mock me," she went on. "Mockery is the one thing a woman cannot accept, or forgive. She can stand any amount of ill-treatment and cruelty, in a sufficient cause. But she cannot be mocked in any cause whatever. You made me certain promises, which honor bound you to fulfil—and then flung your renunciation of them in my face, before strangers who understood. It was a very mean and low-down thing to do."

A faint, sneering smile passed over his face. Her voice hardened.

"I am not a woman to defy—and I am still less a woman to mock. You are going to keep your promises."

"I'll see you in hell first!" he retorted brutally.

She laughed. "You will not see me in hell first," she said calmly. "You may quite possibly see me in hell after—because if there is a hell we shall certainly meet there. But in the meantime—you are going to redeem your word."

He made a slow gesture round the black room.

"You come to me now ... within a few hours...."

"Why not?" she returned hardly.

"Almost before her body is cold...."

She shrugged her shoulders.

"Christine Manderson was an incident," she said indifferently. "A disagreeable episode. She merely infatuated you, as she might have infatuated any man. She has passed."

"Passed," he muttered. "Passed...."

"I do not profess to equal her in appearance," she admitted. "But I am not repulsive. I am considered to be extremely good-looking, and I am much more interesting to talk to than she was. Also, I am well-bred. Most people would find the balance in my favor. But, even if you do not, the difference can only be very small. You will have to make the best of it."

"Or else?" he snarled.

"Or else, if you prefer it, I will exchange your promises for the secrets of this house—with no undertaking to keep them."

He sat biting his nails in the suppression of his rage. She languidly corrected the folds of her dress, leant back in a charming

90

attitude, and waited with unassailable self-possession. The silence was long.

"How much do you want?" he demanded, at last.

"I am not asking you for money," she replied coldly.

"I am offering it unasked," he retorted. "How much do you want?"

"If you had offered to buy back your promises a week ago," she said, "I might have sold them to you. I do not know that I particularly looked forward to their fulfilment. But you flaunted another woman in my face."

"Put it all in the bill," he said coarsely.

"Therefore I will give you nothing back. You shall have only your bond."

"Why waste your breath on heroics to me?" he sneered. "You would sell your soul for money. You have often boasted it."

"I would sell my soul for money any day," she agreed frankly— "but not my pride. I am too much of a sinner already to scruple over the disposal of my soul. But it would not profit me to gain the whole world, and lose my pride."

"Bosh!" he said contemptuously. "Pride pays no bills—and you owe too many to let it deprive you of the pleasure of getting rid of a few."

"That is as it may be," she returned. "I have told you the only exchange I will make."

He sprang up again. This time his anger was scornful.

"Fool!" he cried harshly. "Take your warning! Do you think my secrets—if I have any—are for you? Or that I, myself, am for you? Why do you try to force yourself on to dangerous ground? There are things in the world into which it is not good to pry."

"Plenty," she said, unmoved.

"I may have made you careless promises," he admitted. "I have made many women promises. It is a bad habit. I cannot keep them. I cannot, and will not, marry you, or any other woman. The only one I might have married ... is dead."

"Again you throw her in my face," she murmured, through closed teeth.

"I daresay I used you meanly," he acknowledged. "I did use you meanly. It was not the game to do what I did that night. I freely admit it. And I offer you reparation—the only reparation I can make. It would be the wisest act of your life to take it."

"You have heard my conditions," she replied. "I shall not change them. Unlike most women, I have been gifted with the faculty of being able to make up my mind. The time for compromise has passed."

91

"You don't care for me," he persisted. "You couldn't care for any man. You're not capable of it. It's not in you."

"Whether or not I care for you does not enter into the matter at all," she rejoined calmly. "My capability for affection has no bearing on the present question."

"You were relying on marrying me to pay your debts," he declared. "You could not have built a more forlorn hope. I should not pay your debts if I did marry you. I will give you five thousand pounds for your lie this morning."

She was very angry. The insult dashed all the color from her face, leaving it white and set in lines that made her look almost old. Her eyes glittered menacingly.

"You dare," she said slowly, "to offer me five thousand pounds?"

"And consider yourself damned lucky!" he retorted.

He took out his case, and lit a cigarette with a show of indifference.

"I am not bound to offer you anything," he said carelessly. "That small point seems to have escaped you. You have no claim on me. I consider my suggestion an exceedingly generous one. You can take it or leave it. It's all you'll get."

She rose.

"You insult me again," she said, in measured tones. "You are not wise."

He laughed easily.

"My dear Phyllis," he said, "you are adorable in a rage—but I am afraid I must steel myself against your gentle exactions. Let me convince you that I am really treating you in a highly preferential manner. During my career three women have attempted to blackmail me. They were all ugly—so they got nothing. You are charming—so you get five thousand pounds. That is the most I have ever paid for my smaller indiscretions. And I take the liberty of thinking it more than sufficient compensation for the few erroneous impressions I may have allowed you to contract."

"You are making the mistake," she said, in the same controlled tones, "of imagining that you are buying back your promises to me, which I can quite understand that you value lightly. But I have told you that those promises are not for sale. You have wandered from the real issue. You are not buying the promises of your heart—you are buying the secrets of your house. Are they not on a different scale of values?"

"You know nothing of my house," he returned. "You do not know whether there are secrets in it or not."

"I don't know," she confessed candidly. "Possibly there are not.

But I am prepared to take a sporting chance that there are. And if I am wrong—so much the better for you."

He was silent, looking at her thoughtfully, as if carefully weighing his course of action.

"You were under the suspicion of Scotland Yard," she reminded him, "until I told my lie. You will be under it again if I admit my lie. Inspector Fay would certainly not rest until he had thoroughly investigated your reasons for giving a false account of yourself. He is by no means a fool—and I very much doubt that he is to be bought, anyway so reasonably as I am."

Copplestone's face wore a strange expression. There was now no animosity in it, but rather a mild resignation, in strange contrast to his previous anger.

"So," he said, after a pause, "you would put them on to me again...?"

"I need not have taken them off you," she replied.

"I have offered you five thousand pounds for that," he said slowly.

"I have refused them."

"Think over it well," he advised her impressively.

"I do not need to," she returned.

For a moment they faced each other steadily.

"You mean that—finally?" he asked.

"Finally," she answered.

He moved to a door at the further end of the room, and opened it.

"Come," he said quietly. "You have gone too far to draw back. You shall see the secrets of my house. Follow me."

Chapter XXIV

The Secret of the House

She followed him out of the black room into a dark, narrow passage.

Her calmness and self-possession remained undisturbed. Without a tremor she accepted this unexpected invitation to the secrets of the Crooked House—quite ignorant of, and indifferent to, the danger to which she might be committing herself. That there were hidden things in the house she had for a long time been convinced, but of their nature she had been unable to form even a conjecture, in spite of many attempts to creep into the mystery. Copplestone's sudden decision to reveal them to her was a surprise, and an unpleasant check to the development of her schemes. Either he placed a much lower value on his secrets than she had expected, or her participation in them was by no means to be dreaded to the extent that she had relied upon. In any case her position was considerably weakened, and the success of her plans was no longer the assured thing she had believed it to be.

In silence they ascended a flight of stairs, and reached a door which appeared to be the entrance into a separate part of the building. It was a massive oak door, fitted with double locks of remarkable strength for a private house. Copplestone held it open, motioning her to pass before him, and relocked it on the other side. She was still without any nervousness, but her curiosity increased with every step. He led the way on, and she followed him unhesitatingly. They traversed several corridors, and turned many corners. Her sense of direction told her that they had entered an extreme wing of the house, hidden away among the thickest trees of the garden, and to all appearances unused. The place was damp, dusty, and silent, with the intense silence of emptiness. Some of the doors were open, showing unfurnished, neglected rooms. The papers were peeling off the walls; the fittings were covered with the rust and dirt of years; the soiled blinds half covered the closed, uncleaned windows. The atmosphere was close and unhealthy.

"What a parable of waste!" she said.

He did not reply. They came to a square landing, and another heavy door faced them. Copplestone stopped, and for a moment stood looking at her intently. She did not flinch. He shrugged his shoulders, and took a key from his pocket. It was a peculiar key, and was attached to a strong chain. He fitted it into the lock, and opened the door. Then he turned to her again, and she saw a change coming over his face.

"Go in," he said curtly.

She hesitated, for the first time. He withdrew the key, and returned it to his pocket.

"You need not be afraid," he said.

"I will follow you," she returned, watching him carefully.

He shrugged his shoulders again, and went into the room. She entered after him.

It was a long, low room. There was a window at the far end, but it was so dirty, and the curtains in front of it were so thick and discolored, that the place was in semi-darkness, and the air overwhelmingly heavy and unwholesome. There was a little rough furniture, a strip of worn carpet on the floor, and some untasted food on the table—but it was not any of those dismal objects that attached the woman's gaze. It was rather a white, pasty face that seemed to gleam at her from the darkest corner of the room—the drawn pallid face, and dull lifeless eyes, of a white-haired man, who was sitting in a huddled, contorted attitude on a bare wooden chair.

She shrank back with a startled exclamation, and turned to Copplestone. His face was convulsed with fury, his eyes aflame with hatred.

"Well?" he said harshly.

She drew away from him fearfully.

"What wickedness is this?" she shuddered.

"None of mine," he answered.

The vacant eyes rested on them with a fixed stare, completely devoid of intelligence. The huddled figure evinced no sign of life. It appeared to be unconscious of their presence. Copplestone advanced a few paces; but the woman hung back, horrified.

"Is that ... a living thing?" she whispered.

He laughed—an unnatural, metallic laugh.

"Yes," he said—"it's living ... with as much life as its sins have left it, and its rotten body can hold."

He turned back to her.

"Come nearer," he said. "There is nothing to be afraid of."

But the glassy stare of the motionless figure had unnerved her. She was white, and shaking.

"No, no," she muttered, shrinking further back.

He seized her arm.

"I warned you," he cried roughly, "but you wouldn't listen. You were brave enough then—when you thought I daren't stand up to you. You shall learn your lesson—you who talked so glibly of my secrets. Come closer."

He dragged her with him towards the corner.

"Look!" he commanded. "Look at that thing in front of you—that thing crouching there like an ape. It was once a man. It was once an active, intelligent, healthy human being—a strong handsome member of a strong handsome family. Everything was in its favor. There were no obstacles in its path. It had many more natural gifts than the average man is endowed with. It might have ruled an empire. It might have loaded its name with honor, and left it to its children. It had the capability, the power, and the opportunity to leave the world a better place than it found it. Look at it now."

She stood silent, her head turned away. He went on, with increasing rage.

"Look at that man now! He has brought himself to a state of gibbering insanity by a life of indulgence in every form of vice and depravity known to humanity. He knowingly and deliberately drained his mental and physical resources by every insult to nature that depraved men and women—the lowest creatures of the earth— have devised for the satisfaction of their diseased senses. He was a drunkard and drug-fiend before he was twenty. Every effort was made to check and reclaim him, but he defied them all. He was fully warned. He knew what the consequences would be. He knew that nature cannot be violated continuously without exacting her penalty, sooner or later. But he plunged on. Step by step he brought himself to this. His brain and his body are decaying from the unnameable excesses he has committed with both. He is literally rotting in front of us at this moment."

She put her hands up to her face.

"Can he hear you?" she gasped.

"I don't know," he replied savagely. "Perhaps he can. I hope he can. I hope he can hear every word. It wouldn't be the first time he had heard the story of his shame. And it won't be the last. Curse him!"

She tried to draw him back.

"Come away," she cried. "How can you stand in front of the poor creature, and talk like that before his face?"

His iron grip closed on her wrist, and held her helpless.

"Why not?" he demanded, with dreadful bitterness. "Why should he be spared because he is suffering a fraction of the just and natural consequences of his own deliberate acts? What is there to pity in that? It is a merciful retribution. If you have any sympathy to show—show it to me."

96

"To you?" she echoed.

"To me," he repeated.

She screamed, and tried to wrench herself from his grasp. The horrible head had begun to move slowly from side to side. A faint, ghastly smile appeared round the twisted lips.

"Let me go," she cried. "It's too dreadful."

He dragged her round again.

"You forced yourself into my secrets," he said hardly. "It is too late to shrink back now. You shall know them to the full—and then you may go."

He paused, still holding her. In her horror, and under the sickly, stifling atmosphere of the room, she was almost fainting. But he paid no heed to her condition. His eyes were fixed malignantly on the grinning object of his hatred.

"That man," he said slowly, "was free from any hereditary weakness. His viciousness was not inherent. He came of a good, clean stock. When he was thirty—although the inevitable results of his violations had already seized upon him—he committed the crime of marrying. It was the foulest sin of his life. He knew what the result would be—what it was bound by every natural law to be. He knew that the sins of the fathers must be visited on the children"—he clenched his hands, and she winced as her wrist was crushed in his grip—"and knowing that, he dared to marry."

His voice rose. His face began to work with passion.

"He married a good woman—who bore all the cruelties he heaped upon her because she loved him. Her money had been his only consideration—and when he had got all that he treated her like dirt. But there are limits even to what a woman can bear. He broke her heart, and she died ... mad. If only she had died a little sooner...."

She steadied herself with an effort.

"Who is he?" she asked. "Why is he here, in your house?"

A flood of fury shook him.

"His name is Oscar Winslowe," he said fiercely. "He is my father."

She uttered a sharp cry, and wrenched her hand away from him.

"Your father? That creature ... your father...."

"Yes," he cried wildly—"he is my father. I am George Copplestone Winslowe. Do you wonder that I hate him? I am the victim of his vices—the heir to his sins. He has left me the legacy of outraged nature. I am mad."

She recoiled from him, panting. He was beside himself. His face was distorted; madness glared in his eyes. Then, suddenly, the paroxysm left him. He turned to her weakly, with the appeal of his utter despair.

"Pity me," he said. "Oh, if you are capable of pitying anything in this dreadful world, pity me! My awful inheritance is closing in on me. Every day one more grain of reason leaves me. Like him, I might have been a leader of men. Like him, I have power and capability. I have a brain that could have raised me to the greatest heights. I have a body that can bear any strain. But I am mad."

His agony was pitiful. He sobbed, wringing his hands.

"I can feel the hideous thing growing in me, hour by hour—a little more—a little more. I can feel its clutch tightening on me. And I can't resist. I can't escape. The little mental balance I have is being dragged away from me. In a few years—if I let myself live to it—I shall be a babbling maniac. Nothing can save me. I knew it when I was a boy—before that thing there completely lost its reason. I knew I was born a madman for my father's sins. It crept on me gradually—one sign after another—one horrible secret impulse after another. The slow, sure growth of madness." He buried his face in his hands. "Oh, God! Oh, God!"

In the silence that followed the figure on the chair straightened itself with a jerk, and gibbered at him, twitching spasmodically. The woman turned away, shaking.

"I live in hell," he moaned—"in all the torment of the uttermost hell. I fly from one thing to another for respite, for relief—but there is no relief. I can only make madness of them all. Everything twists and turns in my hands. I can keep nothing straight." Then another gust of passion seized him. He shouted, beating his hands together. "What right," he cried furiously, "have men and women to marry and bequeath disease and madness to their children? What right have they to propagate the rottenness of their minds and bodies? It's worse than murder. It's the cruelest, the most wicked, of all crimes. What are the feelings of a child to such parents? Is it not to hate them—as I hate that foul thing there?—to curse them, as I curse him, with every breath?" His arms dropped limply to his sides. "What is the use of hating?" he said dully. "It can't cure me. It can't cure me."

He looked at her fixedly.

"Well?" he asked bitterly. "You know the secrets of my house. Are you satisfied?"

She laid a hand on his arm, and turned him gently towards the door. There were tears in her eyes.

"Come away," she said weakly. "Let us speak somewhere else."

He followed her. They went out, without another look at the figure behind them, and returned in silence to the black room.

Chapter XXV

Truer Colors

A great change had come over her. All the hardness had disappeared from her face. It was transformed by a wonderful new pity—a latent compassion, stirred for the first time by this miserable man's utter tragedy. And so transformed she was very lovely—with a loveliness that all the arts of an accomplished society woman had never bestowed upon her.

"Forgive me," she said gently. "I would not have said what I did if I had even thought ... of that."

He looked down at her, a world of agony in his tortured eyes.

"Well," he asked—"do you still want to marry me ... now?"

For an instant the old hardness flashed back.

"You would have married her," she returned.

"I wonder," he said slowly. "I wonder ... if I should."

His gaze wandered vacantly round the room.

"She intoxicated me," he said. "Her memory intoxicates me still. She set fire to all my passions. She made me forget the barrier. But I think I really hated her. Perhaps ... if she hadn't died in the garden ... I might have killed her...."

The madness was leaving him, and the weakness of reaction taking its place. He put a hand on her shoulder, and leant heavily on her. His face was mild and kind—the face of the normal man.

"Phyllis," he said softly, "I mocked you, and treated you badly. But it wasn't really I. Forgive a poor madman the sins of his madness."

She made no attempt to check her tears. He took her hand, as gently as a child.

"Don't cry," he begged. "See—I am all right now. Sit down, and let us talk."

Still leaning on her, he moved to a couch, and drew her down beside him.

"First," he said, "I will tell you why I lied to Inspector Fay. I did not go into the house to fill my cigarette case. I was mad. It came on me—as it often does—when I see sane people about me—a rush of hatred and despair."

He spoke dispassionately, without a trace of the terrible disorder that had possessed him a few minutes before. Only the gloom remained—the shadow that never left him.

"You can understand," he went on, "what my life has been since this cloud first settled on me. I tried to fight against it—but how could I fight against a thing that I knew to be there, creeping on me day after day—when I knew that in the end I must give way? Every hour seemed to bring some fresh proof of the madness that was in me—some proof that made resistance more and more futile and hopeless. A thousand times I have been tempted to kill myself—but always there was the dim, desperate hope that some miraculous twist of sanity might yet deliver me. I can't convey to you a tenth—a hundredth—part of the agony of that struggle. There were times when I shrank into the farthest corner of my darkest cellar, and prayed, as only a madman could pray, to be spared from the unjust curse. There were times when I stood out on the roof of my house, and defied the God I had prayed to...."

He stared straight out in front of him, a figure of unutterable pathos—a helpless accuser of Eternal Laws.

"If I were suffering for a fault of my own, I would bear my punishment uncomplaining. But I am innocent. I have done nothing to deserve this torture. And there is always the thought of what I might have been—of what I know I could have been. That is the cruelest torment of all. I have to see sane men and women wasting every minute of their lives—without the slightest appreciation of the value, or the responsibilities, of reason—who might as well be mad, for all the use they are to their fellow-creatures. And I...." He broke off. "That is enough about myself," he said. "I want to talk about you."

He looked at her in surprise, as if noticing the alteration in her for the first time.

"How changed you are," he said. "You have never looked like that before. You have always been so hard. Why have you never looked like that before?"

She was silent. She bent her head, as if ashamed of betraying herself.

"Was all that hardness ... only a cloak ... to hide yourself?"

He seized her hand tightly.

"You fool! You fool!" he cried—"to make yourself hard and unfeeling and unnatural—to try to stamp all the heart out of your life—to blaspheme your sex. Don't you know that a hard woman is the most terrible thing in the world? Don't you know that while men dare to think that they have the image of God, it is women who can really have the heart of God? And to think that all the time you have disguised yourself, you have been capable of looking like that."

"I have been up against the world," she said. "I have never had enough money to be soft-hearted. No woman with feeling can get five hundred per cent. out of her income."

"What does it matter," he returned, "if she can get five hundred per cent. out of life?"

He still held her hand, his eyes fixed longingly on her face.

"If only I were not mad," he said, with all his sadness—"now I know that you are really a woman...."

"Let me go," she said brokenly, withdrawing her hand from his.

"Not yet," he returned, detaining her. "There is something more I want to do." He paused. "My dear," he said softly, "an hour ago I would not have married you even if I had been sane. Now I want to marry you although I am mad. But, since that cannot be, there is something else." He released her, and stood up. "I want you always to look like that," he said. "I want you to forget that you have ever tried to disguise yourself. I want to make it possible for you to go through the rest of your life with your heart in its proper place."

He took his check book from his pocket.

"No, no," she said quickly—"not that."

"Please," he insisted.

"I would have taken it before," she said, forcing back her tears. "But not now."

"You must," he declared. "My money is no use to me. I can't do anything worth doing with it. With all my fantastic extravagancies, I only spend a small part of my income. The rest has been accumulating for years. I shall never use it, and when I die it will pass to some one I have never seen. It is doing no good—and I want it to do some good. What better thing could I do with it than give it ... to the woman I would marry if I could?"

She sprang up.

"For God's sake," she cried, "don't say that! I can't bear it!"

He laid a hand again on her shoulder.

"Do you care?" he asked slowly. "I don't think you cared before. I thought you were only sorry for me now. Do you really care?"

"I do care!" she cried recklessly. "I care—and care—and care. My God, how I care!"

He turned his face upwards, and over it passed a dreadful, mocking smile.

"O God of Mercy!" he muttered—"another torment!"

He drew away from her.

"I shall do this for you," he said firmly. "I intend to do this. And then we must not see each other again. I hope that when you marry, as you must, you will marry a good, clean man—a man who can stand out among his fellow-creatures, and need not shrink away

101

from them, as I must. I want you to be very happy and bring happy children to the world...." His voice shook. "And forget there are unfortunate people in it ... who may only gaze hungrily over the gulf that they can never cross."

He left her sobbing, and went to his writing table.

"No one will know," he said. "I will draw it to myself. The bank is quite close here. I will walk there and cash it at once."

He wrote the check, and rose.

"Wait for me here," he said. "I shall only be a few minutes." And he went out with the face of a stricken man.

Chapter XXVI

Providing for the Worst

Though Inspector Fay had disclosed no more than was necessary for the purpose of the initial charge, the arrest of James Layton was popularly considered to have solved the mystery of the murder of Christine Manderson.

No one realized more fully than Layton himself the overwhelming strength of the case against him. He was as good as condemned already. Beyond his own assertion of innocence, he was utterly defenseless against a sequence of evidence that might well have shattered the strongest reply. And he was without any reply at all, except his own denial. He could only admit the truth of the damning train of circumstances, in face of which his mere word was hopelessly—and, he was compelled to acknowledge, justly—inadequate. The secret of his identity—most crushing fact of all—was lost. He was the Michael Cranbourne whom Christine Manderson, then Thea Colville, had drawn on to ruin and disgrace. He had threatened her, in the presence of witness, with just such an end as she had met with. He had been seen lurking in the garden at the time of the crime. He had been beside himself. And to all that he had no more convincing answer than the plea of not guilty. He placed himself, quite dispassionately, in the position of his own judge and jury. There could be only one result.

The strange message of hope, brought to him by Jenny West, from a mysterious foreigner who had declared knowledge of his innocence and of half the truth, aroused his curiosity, if no more. That one person, at all events, had discovered, and was apparently pursuing, an alternative to his own guilt was interesting, if a slender encouragement to build on. He was not disposed to cling to flimsy hopes. He accepted his position with perfect calmness. Since the confession of his identity to Inspector Fay a load seemed to have been lifted from his mind, and with it had passed the revival of mad passion which the sight of Christine Manderson's fatal beauty had aroused. He found himself able to dwell on her memory—even to contemplate her death—with a cold detachment which surprised himself. He no longer shrank from conjuring up her image—but now it was a dead image from a dead world. And—not without surprise also, and perhaps a certain satisfaction—he found himself looking forward to a visit from Jenny West.

She came to him at the appointed time. She was very white. The deep shadows of sleepless grief and anxiety were round her eyes—but in them shone the fire of a dogged, dauntless courage. Her great untamed soul was aflame with revolt against the implacable circumstances that had placed the man whose name a thousand had blessed on the highroad to the gallows. She threw herself against the wall of facts with all the force of her primitive love. She was one of those whose trust rises to its greatest heights when opposed to reason.

He greeted her kindly. He was cheerful and composed. He showed that he was glad to see her.

"We shall save you, Jim!" she declared, straining back the tears that sprang to her eyes at his kindness. "I know we shall! I know it!"

"God will save His workman," he returned quietly—"if it is His will."

He looked at her closely. And something very like affection came into his face.

"You are pale," he said. "You are over strained. You haven't slept."

She bent her head, to hide her brimming eyes.

"My child...." he said gently.

"What does it matter," she sobbed, "if I haven't slept? How can I sleep—when you are ... here?"

"Listen, my dear," he said—"we must face this thing squarely. It's no use trying to shut our eyes to the truth, however unpleasant it may be. As the case stands at present, no jury in the world could acquit me. I have no reply to the charge, except to declare that I did not kill Christine Manderson—and that will not help me. The evidence is more than enough to satisfy any impartial, clear-thinking man or woman. It would satisfy me. That I know myself to be innocent will not assist me to establish my innocence. Thousands of things may happen in the meantime—but I must prepare to suffer the penalty for a crime that I did not commit."

"You shall not!" she cried passionately. "If there is justice in heaven or earth, you shall not!"

"I do not cling to life," he returned. "It has very little to give me, or to take away. Men may find me guilty—but I shall stand before God innocent. It will not be the first time I have stood before God."

A spark of his old fanaticism flashed into his eyes for a moment, then faded.

"I shall be ready," he said steadily, "for whatever He sends."

"Men shall not find you guilty," she declared. "There are three people working for you. The truth will be discovered."

104

"Your mysterious Frenchman?" he smiled. "What has he done?"

"I don't know," she confessed. "He tells me nothing—except to keep on promising that you will be saved. And that is enough for me."

A frown darkened Layton's face.

"I wish you would not put yourself so completely into the hands of a stranger," he said doubtfully. "Who and what, is this man? And how does he come to be mixed up in this affair?"

"I know nothing whatever about him," she replied. "But there is something that makes me trust him. I believe he will keep his promise."

"I don't like it," he insisted.

"If I didn't help him," she said, "I could do nothing. And I should go mad."

"What has he given you to do?" he asked.

"I promised not to tell any one," she hesitated.

He shrugged his shoulders.

"You had better tell me. You have no one else to protect you."

"It is something I can't understand," she said slowly. "This morning I had to write out the names and addresses of all the Art and Picture Dealers from the Directory, and this afternoon I am to go round in a car to as many of them as I can, with a letter from the French Embassy, to ask if any articles have ever been supplied to, or orders taken from, a Miss Masters, of 35, De Vere Terrace, Streatham, and if so, what."

Layton stared at her in astonishment.

"What possible connection can that have with the case?" he exclaimed.

"I don't know," she said again. "I've tried to think."

"The French Embassy," he mused. "That is strange...."

He checked himself, and looked at his watch.

"You time is nearly up," he said. "Listen to me carefully. There is one very important thing that I want you to understand. Whatever may develop in the meantime, I intend to prepare for the worst."

He kept her silent with a firm gesture.

"My work must go on. No matter what happens to me, my work must go on. And it must be carried on as I have begun it, by some one who has worked with me, and understands my objects—by some one who is human, and unlimited by sect or creed. I don't want to make people religious—it would spoil most of them. I want to make them healthy and happy. I would rather they were clean pagans than unclean Christians. No soul is saved or lost because it happens to take a certain view of the Mysteries of God. It is the bodies I care for—the bodies I want to build. Humanity should be a song of thanksgiving, not a prayer for alleviation."

The fires kindled again. His face was lit up.

"You must continue my work. If I should have to leave it ... you will find everything yours. There is over a million. Use it as I have taught you. Use it to help children to grow into men and women, and men and women to grow into old men and women. Use it to help human beings against the cruelties they inflict on each other— and animals against the cruelties inflicted on them. Promise me that if the worst happens, you will go on where I leave off."

Tears blinded her. She could not speak.

"Promise," he insisted.

"I will," she sobbed. "I will go on—as long as I can live after you."

He stood still, looking at her fixedly. There was the dawn of an awakening on his face.

"My God!" he whispered, "I was wrong. I do cling to life. I want to live. O God, save me!"

And the girl uttered a great sigh of thankfulness, and fell fainting against the wire partition that stood between them.

Chapter XXVII

The Disappearance of Tranter

At one o'clock on the following day, Monsieur Dupont sat in his room waiting for Tranter. At half-past one he had become impatient. At two he seized the telephone directory, and, a minute later, the instrument. At two-thirty he obtained his number.

The answer to his first question stiffened him into an attitude of rigid tensity.

"Mr. Tranter is not in, sir," a voice told him. "He has disappeared."

"Disappeared?" Monsieur Dupont echoed sharply.

"We do not know what has happened to him. He went out last night at nine o'clock, and has not returned."

"Not returned...." the listener muttered.

"We are getting anxious," the voice went on. "He left orders for his supper, and there is no doubt that he intended to return. We have telephoned to the hospitals and the police stations, but nothing has been heard of him. Do you happen to know where he was going?"

There was a moment's pause. Monsieur Dupont's hands were clenched so tightly round the instrument that the veins stood out on them like cords.

"Yes," he said slowly, "I know where he was going."

He rose quickly.

"I will find him," he promised and rang off.

He replaced the instrument, and stood still. For the first time since his arrival in London fear found a place in the expression of his face.

"Dieu," he whispered—"that Crooked House...."

He seized his hat and stick, and hurried out to his car.

Remarkable changes were in progress when he arrived at the Crooked House. A small army of workmen swarmed over the whole place in a condition of feverish energy. There were stacks of tools, dozens of machines, and cartloads of material. At first sight it might have appeared as if nothing less than the effects of an earthquake could have been in process of repair—but, as Monsieur Dupont stood staring about him in amazement, it became apparent that the men were engaged in eliminating the crookedness of the garden, and must have been so engaged from a very early hour. Many of the twisting paths had been shorn of their high maze-like walls of hedge, and the paths themselves were in varying stages of conversion or disappearance. Under rapid and ruthless hands straightness was already appearing out of the confusion. Monsieur Dupont looked positively frightened.

"Mon Dieu," he exclaimed aloud, "they are making it a human garden!"

The house itself presented a no less startling aspect. It was no longer gloomy, deserted, and silent. It was teeming with life. Every window was open, and from within came sounds of rapacious cleaning. A hundred painters had commenced a vigorous assault upon the exterior, and representatives of every branch of house decoration were attacking the interior. It was a scene of resurrection.

Monsieur Dupont almost ran to the open front door. Copplestone's manservant was at work in the hall, and came forward with a sphinx-like expression.

"Mr. Copplestone?" said Monsieur Dupont.

"Mr. Copplestone is away, sir."

"Away...?"

"He left in the car early this morning, sir, without saying where he was going or when he would be back."

Monsieur Dupont was plainly staggered.

"Was he alone?"

"I do not know, sir."

"You do not know?"

"I did not see him leave, sir. He gave me my instructions in the library, and ordered me to remain there until he had gone."

Monsieur Dupont took a threatening step towards him.

"Where is Mr. Tranter?" he demanded, with sudden fierceness.

The man met his challenging gaze steadily.

"Mr. Tranter, sir?"

"Mr. Tranter came here last night—between ten and eleven o'clock."

"I think you must be mistaken, sir. If he had come here, I should have seen him."

Monsieur Dupont clenched his fists.

"I am not mistaken! I say that he came here last night!"

"I did not see him, sir."

"Since then he has disappeared. He has not returned to his house, and nothing has been heard of him. Where is he?"

"I know nothing of Mr. Tranter, sir."

"That is not true!" Monsieur Dupont almost shouted.

"Sir!"

"I say that is not true!"

The man drew himself up.

"It certainly is true, sir."

"It is not! Will you tell the truth to me—or to the police?"

"I have nothing to tell," the man insisted doggedly.

Monsieur Dupont appeared to be beside himself.

"Dieu!" he cried, "if any harm has come to Mr. Tranter, you shall pay for it—all of you!"

The man shrugged his shoulders.

"I can only repeat, sir, that I have not seen Mr. Tranter, and that, so far as I know, he has not been to this house. He is certainly not here now. You are welcome to search every room for him if you like. Mr. Copplestone left word that the house was to be open to any one who might wish to go over it."

"He said that?" Monsieur Dupont exclaimed, his anger giving place to astonishment.

"Yes, sir."

Monsieur Dupont turned away without another word, and walked slowly to the gates. Reaching them, he stopped, and looked back.

"In the name of heaven," he muttered, "what happened in that house last night?"

He went back to his car. Amazement and anxiety were blended on his face. It was plain that his calculations had received an unexpected check, the meaning of which he could not at present grasp. The sudden transformation of the house and garden was a development that had not entered into his scheme of procedure. It presented him with an entirely new and unlooked-for problem. After a moment's indecision, he took out his pocket-book, referred to an address, and gave it to his chauffeur.

During the return journey he sat with his face between his hands, buried in thought. When the car stopped before a house in Grosvenor Gardens, he lifted his head slowly and heavily, as if rousing himself from a stupor.

"Mrs. Astley-Rolfe, if you please," he said to the footman who answered his summons.

"Mrs. Astley-Rolfe is not at home, sir."

"It is most important," said Monsieur Dupont. "I wished to speak to her of a matter connected with Mr. George Copplestone."

"She went away early this morning, sir."

"Away?" Monsieur Dupont repeated.

"With Mr. Copplestone."

Monsieur Dupont started back.

"With Mr. Copplestone?"

"Yes, sir. Just before eight o'clock."

"With Mr. Copplestone...."

"He came in his car, sir, and insisted on Mrs. Astley-Rolfe getting up to see him. She went away with him ten minutes afterwards, without telling us where she was going or when to expect her back."

Monsieur Dupont's face had become blanker and blanker. He stared at the man speechlessly then turned from the door, and gazed in a helpless fashion up and down the street.

"Mille diables!" he murmured, "what does it mean...."

He got into his car again. He looked about him like a man dazed by a heavy blow. Returning to the Savoy, he went up to his room.

There was a telegram on the table. He opened it, and read:

"The name was George Copplestone Winslowe,
Lessing."

Monsieur Dupont uttered an extraordinary sound. In a flash the gloom and uncertainty that had held him gave place to a seething excitement. Crushing the telegram into his pocket, he rushed from the room. Two minutes later he was on his way to Scotland Yard.

Chapter XXVIII

In Pursuit

Inspector Fay was occupied with the arrangement of the evidence to be presented at the inquest on the body of Christine Manderson. He disliked interruptions when at work, but the appearance of Monsieur Dupont banished his annoyance, and called forth a smile of complacent triumph.

"My friend," said Monsieur Dupont, "you know me well enough to be sure that I would not mislead you?"

There was that in the look of him that caused the smile to fade from the inspector's face.

"Of course," he replied, laying down his papers.

"There is not a moment to lose. You must come with me."

"Come with you?"

"Now—immediately."

"But where?"

"Wherever it may be necessary to go. I do not yet know myself. I only know that we must go."

"Impossible," the inspector declared. "I must be ready for the inquest."

"If you do not come with me," Monsieur Dupont retorted, "you will not be ready for the inquest." He allowed his excitement to overflow. "Why do you stand there?" he cried. "I tell you, there is not a moment to lose. Cannot you see that I am serious? In all the years that you have known me I have never been more serious. Come!"

"What for?" demanded the inspector sharply.

"To discover the truth of the death of Christine Manderson."

"The truth is discovered," returned the inspector, looking down at his papers.

"The truth is not discovered," said Monsieur Dupont.

"It is a perfectly clear case," the inspector retorted. "There cannot be the smallest doubt that Layton killed her."

"Layton did not kill her. At the beginning I warned you to ignore the obvious. But you did not. Layton is no more guilty of the crime than you are."

"I am satisfied," the inspector said shortly.

"You must please yourself," said Monsieur Dupont. "I cannot wait. There are two lives to save—his and another. I came here to

111

keep my word to you. I promised that if I succeeded in solving the mystery, I would hand the rest to you. I do not want credit from this affair. There is another meaning in it for me. I am ready to hand the rest to you, if you will come and take it. If you will not come—I must go on to the end myself. The choice is to you."

Inspector Fay looked at him steadily for a moment. Then he turned back to his desk, and locked up his papers.

"I will come," he said.

Chapter XXIX

Ethics of Killing

They swung out from Scotland Yard into Whitehall.

"What has happened?" the inspector asked.

Monsieur Dupont leant forward, controlling his excitement with an effort.

"Mon Dieu," he said, "I wish I knew!"

He took the telegram from his pocket.

"It is an hour only that I have returned from Richmond. I found the house of George Copplestone in course of transformation. I found all the windows open. I found men and women cleaning—painting—making new. I found a hundred men ... making the crooked garden straight."

"Well?" said the inspector—"why not?"

Monsieur Dupont brought his hands together impatiently.

"Why not? There are a thousand reasons why not. But the reason why...."

"Is it an extraordinary thing for a man to open his windows, paint his house, and straighten his garden?"

"It is!" exclaimed Monsieur Dupont. "It is more than an extraordinary thing—it is a gigantic, a brain-splitting thing—if he has kept his windows closed, his house unpainted, and his garden crooked for twenty years. The house of a man is the reflection of his soul. It was the reflection of George Copplestone's soul yesterday. But ... something happened in it last night. And to-day...."

He broke off, and began to smooth out the telegram on his knee.

"The moment I entered that house," he continued, "I knew it was a wicked house. And when that dreadful thing happened, I felt positively that the wickedness of the house had some direct connection with the crime in the garden. I felt that it would be impossible to solve one without solving the other. I knew, also, that you would certainly be satisfied with the evidence against James Layton, and would consider no other possibility. That evidence, I admit, was unanswerable—but I, with some previous knowledge to help me, knew that Layton was innocent. The difficulty in front of me was to prove the guilt of the real criminal in time. My friend Tranter, and that remarkable young protégée of Layton, Jenny West, agreed to help me. Together we began to draw the nets, and the criminal was aware of our movements. In the country yesterday

113

I discovered the identity of the most important witness in the case—but when I went to find her in the evening, she had been snatched away. I instructed Tranter to discover and bring to me the secret of the Crooked House, whatever it might be. He set out to do so at nine o'clock last night. And he has disappeared."

"Disappeared?" the inspector exclaimed.

"Without a trace. I, only, knew where he was going. And not only has he disappeared—but Copplestone and Mrs. Astley-Rolfe have disappeared with him."

Inspector Fay began to show more interest.

"They will be wanted for the inquest," he said sharply.

"If we do not find them in time for the inquest," Monsieur Dupont returned, "there will be two inquests to hold."

"Two inquests?" the inspector echoed.

"I could not understand it," continued Monsieur Dupont. "It was contrary to all my calculations. I was bewildered—and you may recollect that I am not often bewildered. But when I returned to my hotel, I found this." He held out the telegram. "It is the answer to a certain inquiry I have made."

"What does it mean?" the inspector asked, handing it back.

"It means," said Monsieur Dupont slowly, "that we shall be lucky if we find Tranter alive."

"Where can they have gone?"

"I do not know. I can only guess—and if I have not guessed rightly, we shall not see him again."

"Are you telling me," the inspector demanded, "that Copplestone killed the woman he had just become engaged to?"

"I shall tell you who killed her within twelve hours," Monsieur Dupont replied. "I will tell you why she was killed now."

He paused.

"Why," he asked, "did the murderer, whoever it was, kill her so horribly? Why was it not enough to deprive her of life? Could one have desired more? Why was she stamped on, and torn, and crushed?"

"It was obviously done in the madness of jealousy and revenge," replied the inspector.

"It was done in madness," said Monsieur Dupont—"but it was not the madness of jealousy or revenge. It was the madness of a strange and terrible hatred. It was done—because the killer hated her beauty and not her."

The inspector stared at him blankly.

"Hated her beauty, and not her...?"

"Twenty years ago," said Monsieur Dupont, "there was in France

114

a very beautiful woman. She was named Colette d'Orsel. It was said that she was the most beautiful woman in the country. She was also very rich, very generous, and very kind. She was always doing good actions. She had not an enemy in the world. There was no one who could have wished her a moment's pain. She was only twenty-five. With several of her friends she went to stay at Nice. One night she was found in the gardens of her hotel—almost torn to pieces."

"I remember the case," said the inspector. "It was a ghastly affair."

"There appeared no motive. She was wearing some splendid jewels. They had been crushed with her, but nothing was missing— not a stone. She had just returned from the tables, and had not troubled to deposit her winnings of the evening with the cashier of the hotel. Forty thousand francs were found on the body. Not a note had been touched. The greatest detectives of France were called in to solve the mystery—but they solved nothing. They made the mistake of trying to find a motive. They looked for a person who could have had a reason to kill her. But it was time lost. They should have looked among the people who had no reason to kill her. The weeks became months, and still they discovered nothing. That crime is a mystery to-day."

The inspector's attention was rivetted. He remained silent.

"Ten years ago," Monsieur Dupont proceeded, "there was in Boston a young girl named Margaret McCall. She was wonderfully beautiful. Her parents were poor people, and she worked for her living. She was quiet and reserved by nature. She made few friends, and cared little for the society of men. Naturally there were hundreds who regretted, and attempted to overcome, that characteristic; but she went her own way quietly and firmly. One evening her body was found in a lonely part of one of the public parks torn and crushed in the most terrible manner. The police were helpless. The thing that baffled them completely was the absence of any motive for the crime. They tried to find one—but all that they found was what I have said, that she had been a good, honest girl— that she had had no enemies—that she had not jilted a man, or wronged a woman—that she had never flirted, or encouraged men to pay attentions to her. Yet there she had been found—broken and mutilated. The small sum of money she carried had remained untouched. The crime was never solved."

His voice had sunk lower. He had dwelt on each detail with impassive deliberation.

"This week, Christine Manderson—without doubt the most beautiful woman of the three—was found in that crooked garden at

Richmond, if possible in a more horrible condition than either of the others."

"You mean," exploded the inspector, "that the murderer of Colette d'Orsel at Nice twenty years ago also killed Margaret McCall in Boston ten years after?"

"I do," replied the low voice.

"And Christine Manderson here three days ago?"

"And Christine Manderson here three days ago. But this time there was a difference. An unfortunate chain of circumstances provided clear evidence against an innocent man—James Layton. I admit that as the case stood you had no option but to arrest him. But in doing so you committed the same mistake that your French and American brothers had committed before you. They had looked for a motive, and could not find one. You found a motive, and devoted yourself to the man with the motive. You should have looked for the Destroyer."

There was something of awe in the silence that followed, like the hush that succeeds the passing of a storm.

"My friend," said the inspector slowly, "what utterly monstrous thing are you telling me?"

Monsieur Dupont turned to him a face of massive innocence.

"Is it monstrous?" he said mildly. "If a man is born with a longing to kill elephants, he is a daring sportsman. If the longing is to kill beetles, he is a scientist. But if the inclination is to kill men— or women—he is a criminal lunatic. Why? If the desire to kill is not in itself monstrous, the desire to kill a particular thing, whatever it may be, cannot be monstrous. It can only be illegal. If it is dreadful to kill a young child, it must be dreadful to kill anything young. If it is cowardly for a man to kill a woman, it is cowardly for a man to kill the female sex in any shape or form. Yet, what scientist allows the matter of sex to interfere with the impalement of his beetle? Nor would he do so if his hobby were to impale human beings. If he searches for a beautiful beetle to kill, it only requires a broadening of his particular outlook for him to search for a beautiful woman to kill. There may be a perfectly sane and moral country in the world (although I have never heard of it) in which it would be criminal to kill the beetle, and scientific to kill the woman. I confess that a well-mounted collection of beautiful women would be very much more interesting to me than the finest collection of beautiful beetles. But if I have the one, I am made a member of a Royal Society—and if I have the other, I am executed. And the only reason for that is that the human beings make the laws, and not the beetles."

The car swung round a sharp corner, and the inspector's

amazement was interrupted by the sudden necessity of keeping his position. Monsieur Dupont continued slowly.

"But the monstrousness of this case is not that three people have been killed—but that three people have been more than killed. It is monstrous because we have none of the simple dignity of the primitive slayer, and all the morbid excesses of the modern despoiler. While it might be an entirely respectable thing to kill a woman to preserve her beauty, it is an entirely monstrous thing to kill her to destroy it. That is the only reason why the collector of beetles and butterflies is not the most cold-blooded of murderers. That is the only——"

"What in the name of all that's unholy," gasped the inspector, "are you going to say next?"

Monsieur Dupont leant forward as the car stopped, and opened the door.

"Next," he replied gravely, "I am going to inform you that we have arrived at Paddington, and request you to get out."

Chapter XXX

Monsieur Dupont's Task

He bought the tickets, and conducted the inspector to a train.

"Where are we going?" demanded the bewildered officer, as Monsieur Dupont settled himself in a corner, and produced his cigar case.

"We are going," said Monsieur Dupont, "to a delightful little village, hidden away in the hills of the country—far from the sins of cities—where they do not even know that Paris is the center of the world."

Fortunately they had the carriage to themselves. Monsieur Dupont smoked in silence for some minutes.

"I will explain to you," he began, at last, "how I came to be concerned in this affair. The reason was that, after my retirement, I had the honor to marry a cousin of Colette d'Orsel. The brother of my wife had been one of the party at Nice at the time of the crime, and, though there was not the least evidence against him, the police had allowed it to be known that they looked upon him as the guilty person. You know how ready certain people are to discuss and even to credit the wildest theories—and you know also that after sufficient discussion the wildest theories become not only possibilities, but probabilities. The cloud of suspicion hung over him, ruining his health and his life, and casting a shadow over the whole family. When I married my wife, I determined that the shadow should be removed. And for the past two years I have devoted myself to that object.

"You can imagine," he went on, after a pause, "the difficulties that confronted me. Eighteen years had elapsed since the crime had been committed. Men, women, and even buildings, had passed, and been replaced—records had been lost—memories failed. But money, perseverence, and imagination slowly conquered. Step by step the years were overcome. With the aid of a small army of assistants, I succeeded in isolating a certain person. I placed that person beside the dead body of Colette d'Orsel, and began my pursuit. Mon Dieu, how I worked! After the hardest year of my life, I at last established a link between the death of Colette d'Orsel and the death of Margaret McCall—and that link was the personality I had isolated in the first place at Nice. But it had changed itself. I followed scent after scent—trail after trail. When I came to London a few days ago,

118

I had sufficient information to allow me to commence the final stage of the adventure. I had solved the most difficult question of all—the present identity of my quarry. The second most difficult question remained to be solved—proofs of guilt. How could I obtain them? How could I prove that this person—living here in all the security of time—was the person who had torn those two women to pieces in America and France ten and twenty years ago? I had certain clues to follow up, but the results could not possibly have been sufficient to prove such an accusation. What was I to do? To rely upon observation? To search for—and wait for—a proof in this person's daily intercourse with the world? To place a beautiful woman within reach, and watch for a betrayal? That was actually the object in my mind when I called on my friend Tranter, and requested him to open to me the doors of London society. Sooner or later, I should have found, or brought about, the situation I was looking for. It might have been years—doubtless it would have been years—if he had not, by the most remarkable chance, taken me direct to that house at Richmond. Then came the death of Christine Manderson. It was horrible—appalling! And to think that I, who had detected and tracked the Destroyer, had been there in the same garden, within a few yards of the third death, and yet was no nearer my proofs! And to add to my difficulties, there was the certainty that an innocent man would suffer unjustly if I could not succeed in time."

He paused, looking grimly out at the passing scenery.

"And if I had not sent Tranter to the Crooked House yesterday, I do not know how I could have succeeded in time."

He turned abruptly from the window, put his feet up on the seat, and closed his eyes.

"I am a little tired," he said. "If you will excuse me, I will take a nap."

He slept for an hour.

They got out at a small country station. The shadows of the hot twilight were merging into darkness. A few minutes walking brought them to an inn, at which Monsieur Dupont demanded, and obtained, a conveyance.

For half an hour they drove through the heavily scented air of the country. Scarcely a word was spoken until they reached another village. There, Monsieur Dupont requested the inspector to alight and they proceeded on foot.

The red rear-light of a motor-car appeared at the turn of a corner. Monsieur Dupont drew a deep breath.

"Le bon Dieu be thanked!" he muttered.

The car was stationary and empty. Monsieur Dupont laid a hand on the radiator.

"It is hot," he said. "They have only been here a few minutes. Do not make a sound."

He opened a gate. The long low shape of a house was in front of them. They stood still, listening. There was no sound, no light.

"To the back," Monsieur Dupont whispered.

Chapter XXXI

What They Heard

They crept round the house. At the back a pair of French windows were open, but heavy curtains were drawn across them. No light was visible. They listened. A voice was speaking—slowly, scarcely above a whisper, but a whisper of contemptuous pride.

"Yes," it said, "I am the Destroyer! I was born to kill. It was the curse of my birth."

The silence of the room was broken only by the faint sound of a woman sobbing. Monsieur Dupont and the inspector drew nearer to the window.

"You fools!" said the arrogant voice. "What are your laws of Right and Wrong to me? I am Right and Wrong. What are your Codes of Sin? I am Sin. Who are you to judge me? Who are you to set your little laws against My Madness?"

There was a long pause. Then the voice continued, in a tone of dull bitterness.

"Ever since I had strength to break, I have broken—to tear, I have torn. The disease took command of me long before I knew its meaning. When I was a child the sight of pretty things frightened me. I used to shrink from them, and hide my face. I was only quiet and normal when there were plain, colorless things about me. As I grew older the fear developed into hatred—and with hatred grew, slowly and subtly, the inclination to destroy. At first the opposition of all that was normal in me sufficed to keep the desire in check, but day by day it grew stronger and stronger, and day by day the power to resist became less and less. The increase of the hatred into madness followed the growth of the impulse towards the first surrender. It came upon me for the first time when I was twelve. How well I remember that day! My sanity had fought its strongest battle, and my head was still throbbing and swimming with the strain of it. I was taken to a strange house, and left alone in a bright room. On the wall there was a picture of a very beautiful woman. I couldn't take my eyes off it. I couldn't move from in front of it. New passions, that I had never felt before, were tearing me. The picture seemed to be alive, to be mocking me. I hated it. I felt that it was cruel and loathsome—that it had wronged me. My whole body was on fire—my brain was flaming. Then something seemed to snap in my head. I lost myself. Irresistible forces took possession of me, and used me. When I came to myself ... the picture was lying at my feet ... in fragments."

The voice settled down into an expressionless monotone, pursuing its story without emotion.

"From that moment my doom lay on me. I had made the initial submission. Any attempt at resistance after that was futile. I was helpless. Out of my hatred of beauty in any shape or form came the desire to obtain the most beautiful things I could find to enjoy the mad ecstasy of shattering them. I had all the morbid secret longing to induce attacks of my own madness—to enjoy the awful exaltation, the triumph of destruction. I was not ashamed. I found myself entirely without scruple, without conscience, incapable of remorse. When the periods of desire were upon me, I hesitated at nothing to gratify them. At first they were frequent—sometimes there were only a few days between—but as I grew older the intervals lengthened, until sometimes I dared to think myself free. But, sooner or later, it came again. I knew all the warning signals—the creeping in of uncontrollable thoughts—the brain pictures—the quickening of mind and body—then the grip of the madness. All I could do at such times was to collect a number of things sufficiently beautiful to satisfy my lust, and lock myself in to an orgy of destruction. Then I was normal again for another period. So I grew up. When I was twenty, I learnt the truth."

"I told him," a woman's broken voice said. "I hadn't the heart to tell him before. I was hoping against hope that the curse would pass away as he grew into manhood. But when I saw that it would not ... I told him."

"Then I knew there was no escape," the dull voice went on. "The results of my father's vices and my mother's madness were my inheritance. God! ... what a legacy!"

The voice flamed for an instant—then subsided again into its previous monotony.

"The intervals became longer and longer, but each time the madness recurred it tightened its clutches. Each time it made me more and more its own property. Whenever the warnings showed themselves I fled to the refuge of Miss Masters's house. She bought and kept there things on which, when the mania was at its height, it satisfied me to expend my lust. But those inanimate things, though sufficient for that purpose, had no power in themselves to produce an attack of the madness. The capability to do that was reserved to a woman's beauty—the effect of which, so far, I had had no opportunity to experience. That opportunity came to me for the first time at Nice—twenty years ago. I had never seen a really beautiful woman before I saw Colette d'Orsel."

122

Another pause followed the name. The room behind the curtains remained in tense silence until the voice resumed.

"I can remember it now—as if it were yesterday. How she stood there—in the soft shaded light—terribly beautiful. And I—the Destroyer—watched her paralyzed—knowing for the first time the pinnacle of my madness. The sight of her numbed all my sanity. I could no more have torn myself away from that place than I could have resisted the new flood of my disease that broke over me like a nightmare wave. I was introduced to her. As I bent over her hand I almost laughed at the thought of what her horror would have been if she had known the impulses that surged through me. Her voice—the touch of her—burnt into me like flames. I knew what the end would be, but I was powerless in the grip of my inheritance. And she—in the pitiless irony of it—liked me! Three evenings later I met her in the gardens of the hotel. We sat together ... alone for the first time. I struggled. My God, I struggled! But it was useless. The white shape of her next to me—the dim outline of her features—the whole nearness of her beauty.... Then it came on me, as I knew it would— the final rush of irresistible hatred. When I knew myself again ... she was lying on the ground ... smashed ... my first living victim."

The woman sobbed.

"God forgive him!" she cried. "He was innocent himself. It wasn't really him...."

Light footsteps moved across the floor.

"Let me be," said the voice hardly. "What God does with me is for God to do. Sit down again."

The footsteps returned.

"I left her there, and went back to the hotel. I sat down in my room, and analyzed my feelings. The madness had left me. My mind was perfectly clear and steady. I felt no horror at what I had done— no remorse—only a sense of impersonal regret at the death of an innocent woman, and a faint detached pity for her misfortune in crossing my path. I carefully considered my position, and certainty that there could be no evidence against me dispelled any fears for myself—but my cold-blooded sanity realized that the odds were tremendously against a recurrence of the same good fortune, and that the avoidance of the opposite sex must become the chief care of my life. Then I went to bed, and slept soundly. The discovery of Colette d'Orsel's body early the next morning provided the sensation of the year at Nice. The police were confounded. There was no motive—no clue. It is an unsolved mystery to-day."

The callousness of the story was so revolting that even the inspector, seasoned as he was, allowed a muttered expression of disgust to escape him. But Monsieur Dupont remained as silent and still as the house itself.

"Ten years later," continued the voice, "I went to America. For five years I had been free from any return of the madness. You can imagine the longing to be like other men—to presume on the years of immunity. I felt unshakably sane. I even felt that I had never been mad. I gloried in the keenness of my intellect, the absolute order and control of my thoughts. What had I to do with madness? But in Boston ... I saw Margaret McCall. In an instant I was mad. In an instant——"

A cry tore the air—a cry so awful in its inhuman fury that the two listeners shrank back horrified. For a moment the room seethed with confusion. The voices of men and women were blended in rage, terror, and command. Then the curtains were wrenched aside, and two figures rushed out shrieking into the darkness of the garden.

Chapter XXXII

The Beauty-Killer

Four more figures dashed out through the curtains—two women and two men. The inspector and Monsieur Dupont joined them. Guided by the sounds in front of them, they dashed across the garden at the top of their speed.

A black wall of earth loomed up before them, like the rising of a gigantic wave. It was strongly rivetted, and must have been at least ten feet high. It was quite inaccessible from where the pursuers stopped beneath it.

"Look! Look!" a woman screamed.

They looked up.

"My God!" the inspector exclaimed.

On the height above them, silhouetted against the pale sky of the summer night, they saw a figure—its arms uplifted in an attitude of majesty, of triumphant defiance. The white light of the moon lit up a face terrible beyond words in its pride, its sin, and its utter madness.

"I am the Beauty-Killer! I killed Colette d'Orsel! I killed Margaret McCall. I killed Christine Manderson...."

Another figure scrambled up out of the darkness on to the height, and the silver head of Oscar Winslowe gleamed in the light. For a moment he crouched—then sprang forward with a yell. The two figures swayed backwards in a fierce struggle.

"They will go down!" a man's voice cried. "It is the edge of a gravel pit. The fence will not bear. There is a sheer drop of fifty feet."

"Let them go," another woman sobbed. "It is the best way."

And, even as she spoke, there was the sound of tearing woodwork. The struggling figures stood out for an instant with startling clearness—then disappeared like the sudden shutting off of a moving picture. And the whole night seemed to wince at the thud that followed.

"We must go down," the man's voice said, breaking the silence in an awestruck whisper. "There is a way round the other side."

They followed him round the edge of the pit. It seemed like walking round the world. They descended a steep slope—and then, in the vast gray silence, a circle of pale faces surrounded the dead bodies of Oscar Winslowe, and John Tranter.

Chapter XXXIII

Last Truths

"My friends," said Monsieur Dupont, "you have already heard a great part of the story. John Tranter was the son of Oscar Winslowe. He was mad. He was, as he called himself truly, a Beauty-Killer. That strange lust he inherited from his mother, who had been robbed of all she cared for, and hoped for, in life by a beautiful woman, and rendered insane three months before his birth. It was a most pathetic tragedy. We shall now hear——"

"One moment," Inspector Fay interrupted. "As I represent the police here, I should be glad to know, before we go any further, whose house I am in."

"Pardon me," Monsieur Dupont apologized. "I had forgotten. You are in the house of Doctor Lessing," he inclined himself towards the doctor, "who will in due course repeat to you a statement which he made to me yesterday. This lady is Miss Masters, who was Tranter's nurse. Mrs. Astley-Rolfe and Mr. Copplestone—which, I fancy, is not his correct name—you know already."

He added a high compliment to the inspector's present position and past achievements, and then turned to Copplestone.

"Mr. Copplestone, when Tranter did not return to me at the appointed time this afternoon, I went to your house. I found great changes. I found it, as you say, upside down."

Copplestone was radiant with happiness. Every trace of the old gloom had left him. He was a new man.

"I should think you did!" he retorted. "And you'd have found the earth upside down as well, if I'd been able to turn it."

"I was puzzled," Monsieur Dupont admitted. "I could not understand it. But I knew this—that when the shadows roll away from a man's house, they roll away from his life. When he draws the blinds and throws open the windows of his house to the light and the air, he draws the blinds and throws open the windows of his soul. When he straightens his garden, he straightens himself. I knew that before you would lift the cloud from your house something must have lifted the cloud from you. You had been delivered——"

"There was a fellow in the Bible," said Copplestone—"I think he was a king—who was cured of leprosy by taking a dip in a river. I don't know what happened afterwards, but I am quite sure that he turned his palace upside down when he got back."

He sprang up, his face illuminated with all the wonder of his new birth.

"I am free!" he cried. "Free! That's what my house told you. I had been brought out into the light after half a life of darkness. I had been released after forty years of prison, of torment that all the tortures of the Inquisition at once couldn't have equalled!"

He stared about him, like an intoxicated man.

"This room is too small!" he almost shouted. "Everything is too small. I want to dance on the Universe. I want the world to be a football. I want to play enormous games with giants—" He checked himself abruptly, and sat down. "Forgive me," he said. "You would understand, if you knew what I have suffered."

"I can, for one," agreed the doctor heartily.

"And I, indeed," said Monsieur Dupont. "But to proceed with the story—I think it would be better to commence with what Miss Masters has to tell us."

He bowed to a gray-haired, grief-stricken woman. There was a pause before she overcame her emotion sufficiently to speak.

"I took charge of Mary Winslowe's child from its birth," she began, at last. "She entrusted it to me in her sane moments, and I kept my trust faithfully. Perhaps it would have been better if I had not."

"You did your duty," the doctor said.

"It was a condition that he should never come under his father's influence, or even know his real name. He was to be kept in complete ignorance of the tragedy of his birth. It was necessary for him to be christened in his proper name to legalize the inheritance of his mother's fortune, but after that I took him away, and brought him up in strict accordance with my promises. He was told that both his parents had been drowned at sea. I gave him the name of John Tranter—Tranter was an old family name of mine. He was a bonny little fellow. I never thought that he might have inherited his mother's madness."

"The Laws of Nature are inexorable," said the doctor. "If only the Second Commandment were given to people as the Law of Nature instead of the threat of God, it would be of some value."

"I hardly realized it," she went on, "even when the symptoms had unmistakably developed. But it increased too plainly to be denied. I hoped and prayed that the horrible disease would pass away from him as he grew up—but it grew stronger and stronger with him. At last he made me tell him what it really was. It was against my promise, but he had to know. I pledged my word that I would keep his secret, and it was arranged that whenever he felt the approach of an attack he would come to me. I kept things for him. At first smaller things satisfied him. He was content to destroy flowers, pictures, prettily colored china, anything that was beautiful. But after that visit to France, when he was twenty, there was a change. He never told me what had happened—that he had killed a woman—but from that time only a woman's beauty would satisfy him. The attacks became few and far between, but when they came he would have died with the very force of his madness if he had not had some representation of a beautiful woman to expend it on."

"It's frightful—incredible," the inspector exclaimed.

"It was all the more pitiful," she said, "because his sanity was so wonderful. He had a towering intellect. He succeeded in anything he put his hand to."

"He was looked upon as one of the greatest authorities on finance in the country," said the inspector.

"He could have been a Member of Parliament before he was thirty if he had cared for politics. He refused a title. To be a Privy Councillor was the only honor he accepted. And he—one of England's great men—came to my little house at Streatham to gratify his madness to destroy."

She looked round at them defiantly, anger displacing the sorrow on her face.

"But he was not guilty," she declared. "His hands may have killed those three women—but he was not guilty. Nor was that poor innocent woman, his mother, who died in the madhouse. They were both clean of sin. It was on his wicked father that the guilt lay. It was Oscar Winslowe who was responsible for the lives that have fallen to his sins. Oscar Winslowe, and no one else."

"I bear witness to that," agreed Doctor Lessing. "Mary Winslowe was the gentlest, the sweetest, and the most patient woman that ever walked this earth, as you will see when I tell you my story. And he was the biggest blackguard that ever blasphemed the likeness of his Maker."

"It is true," said the woman.

She drew back in her chair, and pressed a hand to her forehead.

"That is all I have to tell you," she concluded.

"Last night," said Monsieur Dupont, "I called at your house, and was told by the lady who lives next door that you had left in a hurry two hours before."

"Yes," she said.

"I presume that you did so on instructions from Tranter?"

"Yes."

"Evidently he shadowed me to Paddington Station, as I expected he would, and decided to remove you in case I should get on the right track."

"He sent me an urgent message," she said, "saying that a great disaster hung over his head, and that I must go away without leaving any trace. He told me where to go, and promised to come to me and explain."

"He knew that it was only you who could give any proof against him?"

"After forty years," she returned, with a touch of bitterness, "he ought to have known that I should not betray him."

"Even if one had told you of those three dreadful crimes that he had committed, and that an innocent man was accused of the last one?"

She locked her hands together.

"Don't ask me," she cried. "I don't know what I should have done."

"He foresaw that problem," said Monsieur Dupont. "His sanity was, as you have said, wonderful. But the sanity of madness is always wonderful—that is why madmen are such superb criminals. It is only a madman who can be really sane. Although I allowed him to see that I knew already something of the truth, he never betrayed himself by even a tremor. He had all the grand egotism of the born criminal. His disguise was impenetrable. He was never sure how far my knowledge went, but not a sign of anxiety did he ever show. We played a game of cross purposes. I used him, under the pretense of requiring his assistance, to keep him by my side, and in the hope that as he saw me draw nearer to him step by step, he would break down. He, on his side, allowed himself to be used in order to keep watch on my moves, and safeguard himself against them, as he did in the case of Miss Masters. He dared not leave me. In all my conversations with him, I placed him more and more at his wit's end to know how much I really knew. As much from curiosity as from anything, I instructed him to discover the secret of Mr. Copplestone's house, for I was convinced that it did contain an interesting secret. He was quite willing to make the attempt. It did not promise to lead me any nearer to him. He little thought when he went—and I had little thought when I sent him—that he was going to his own undoing."

"And my salvation," Copplestone added.

"There," said Monsieur Dupont, "it passes to you to enlighten me."

"First," returned Copplestone, "I should like to know what caused you to be so positive, after being in my house only two or three hours, that there was a secret in it."

"My instinct for the mysterious is seldom at fault," said Monsieur Dupont. "Have you not observed how, by their characters, their habits, and their desires, human beings draw to themselves certain events and conditions of life? And it is equally true that houses draw to themselves certain contents and certain kinds of inhabitants. If a house is particularly adapted to contain a secret, in the course of time will certainly contain one. By a few strokes of his pencil an architect can condemn a house to become the scene of a murder, as surely as he can make it a convenient or inconvenient dwelling. Your house was constructed to hide a secret. And I was not only sure that it did hide one, but that it hid one which was in some way connected with the crime in the garden."

"I have had some experience of that instinct of yours," the inspector remarked, with a somewhat rueful smile.

"Well," said Copplestone, "instinct or no instinct, it certainly did hide a secret, and that secret was that Oscar Winslowe lived in it—if his condition could be called living. For the last five years he had been practically a helpless imbecile. He seldom uttered a sound beyond a gibber, and hardly seemed to be conscious. He was suffering the natural consequences of his vices. He had been gradually reaching that condition since nature had dealt him her first stroke of vengeance more than thirty years ago. One by one his faculties had rotted. He was a living mass of decay."

"It was a sure thing," the doctor said. "Such a condition was bound to come. I prophesied it to his face when I first knew him."

"That was the secret of my house," Copplestone proceeded. "My own secret was that I believed myself to be his son—the inheritor of the curse that really belonged to Tranter. And the horror of it, the helplessness, the constant contemplation of the awful state of the man I knew as my father, and the morbid certainty that sooner or later I must come to the same state, actually drove me to the madness that was not really in me at all."

"But how had you come to believe yourself to be his son?" the inspector asked.

"That was the last of Winslowe's diabolical acts. He inherited a large fortune on condition that a child of his, to whom it could succeed, was alive at the time of the testator's death. He did not know anything of his own child, and did not want to. He was afraid that if he made public inquiries for it, he might learn publicly that it was dead, and lose his claim. Also, he was afraid of other complications and exposures."

"And with good reason," said the doctor grimly.

"He wanted a child of five to produce as his son, George

Copplestone Winslowe—and possibly make away with in due course after the business was settled. I am quite sure that would have been my fate if nature had not come to my rescue by striking him. He knew, from his knowledge of the underworld of London, how such things could be arranged without risk. No doubt he bought me for a few pounds. I am not the first heir to an estate who has been produced by such means."

"True enough," agreed the inspector. "The heir to a million has been bought for a fiver."

"But a few years after taking possession of the fortune, he was struck down, as I have said, by the first instalment of nature's retribution, and was incapable of carrying out his plans. No one cared for me. No one thought of removing me from the sight and influence of his growing imbecility. I was brought up under the shadow of it. And so the horror was born in me—the belief that I was mad. What chance had I to resist it, in those surroundings? When I came to an age to do so, I searched out the story of my birth, of my father's excesses and my mother's madness, and my doom crashed upon me. Can you wonder that I became what I was?"

"No, indeed," said Monsieur Dupont.

"I dropped the name of Winslowe. It was loathsome to me. I used my other two names, George Copplestone. They, at least, had come from my mother's side. My old manservant and his wife stuck to me, and kept my secrets. The income devolved on me in consequence of Winslowe's incapability. And so things went on. In my morbid demoralization I saw myself growing nearer and nearer to that wretched creature day by day."

"Dreadful!" shuddered the doctor. "It must have been a living hell."

"Then, last night, Tranter came. He climbed up on the ivy, and tried to spy into Winslowe's room. But I was there, and heard him. I dragged him in through the window. I suppose it was some look, some likeness to his mother, that stirred Winslowe's memory. He recognized him, and a flash of sanity came back to him. Under that sudden mental stimulation he recovered his power of movement, and was able to confess at least a part of the truth. Tranter was taken off his guard, and I forced him to admit his madness. I compelled him to take Winslowe and myself to Miss Masters, and she, in her turn, brought us here."

"I imagined she would," Monsieur Dupont remarked.

Copplestone drew a deep breath, and laughed aloud.

"And I am like other men! I can live as other men live. I can do what other men do. I can——" His eyes rested on the woman beside

131

him, and his face grew tender. "Yes," he repeated slowly, "I can ... I can...."

There was a pause.

"And it was Tranter who killed Christine Manderson...." the inspector said, almost to himself.

"It was," said Monsieur Dupont. "He admitted to you on the night of the crime that he had known her in America years ago. And here we have a curious study in conflicting emotions. When he first met her, he had already killed two beautiful women. She was certainly more beautiful than either—yet he was able to associate with her on intimate terms for a considerable time, and even to tear himself away from her at last, without adding her to the victims of his madness. How was he able to do that? It was undoubtedly because he loved her. He had not loved either of the other two, so there had been no opposing emotion to his mania. But he loved Christine Manderson, and love was capable of holding the madness in check, because love, in its full strength, is the strongest of all human emotions. Love is stronger than madness, and ten times stronger than sanity. But after he left her the love faded to a certain extent, while the madness increased. Therefore, when he was suddenly confronted with her extraordinary beauty a few nights ago, the love that had faded was unable to restrain the madness that had not. And he killed her."

"My God!" exclaimed Copplestone, "to think that he stood there with us over the body he had torn—and even lifted it into my arms—without so much as a quiver."

"He was not capable of remorse or regret," Monsieur Dupont returned. "If he had been, he would have killed himself long ago." He paused. "There remain now a few points of my own part in this affair to tell you, and we will then ask the doctor for his statement."

"Before you do that," said Doctor Lessing, bluntly, "I, for one, am curious to know who you really are, and how you came to take such a large hand in the whole business."

"My connection with the whole business," replied Monsieur Dupont, "is a long story. I have already told it to Inspector Fay, and I will tell it again with pleasure when all the more important statements have been made. As regards myself——"

Inspector Fay took upon himself the continuation of the sentence.

"Up to a few years ago," he said, "Monsieur Dupont was, under a certain pseudonym, the most brilliant member of the French Secret Service—and was, in fact, admitted to have no equal in the whole of Europe."

"A gross exaggeration, my friends," protested Monsieur Dupont. He waved the inspector to silence. "When I came to London last week," he told them, "I came knowing that John Tranter had killed two women. I had known that when I returned from America six months before. You can imagine the difficulties in front of me then. I was to prove that an English Privy Councillor, a well-known and highly respected man, was in reality a madman who was responsible for two of the most dreadful crimes that had ever been committed. I had never seen him, but fortunately he was in Paris at that time, and I had no difficulty in making his acquaintance. By extreme good fortune, I was able to render him a service in the streets which placed him under an obligation to me. I observed him carefully, only to find him to all appearances the sanest and most level-headed man I had ever met. But there was one thing—he shut himself away completely from the society of women, and he avoided all places where beauty was to be found in any form. But I was so far from any proof. My next step was to test my own belief that his madness was an inherent disease, and to do that I employed inquiry agents in this country to discover whether there were any records of such a case in existence. It is only two weeks since I received information from them that a woman named Mary Winslowe had died in an asylum from that very kind of madness, forty years ago."

"That is true," corroborated the doctor.

"I came to London immediately. While following up my clues, I renewed my acquaintance with Tranter, and pressed him to act as my cicerone in London society, hoping to be able to entrap him into a situation that would lead him to betray himself. And he took me to Richmond. What happened there, you know. Though he knew when Christine Manderson first came into the room what the outcome would be, he was unable to tear himself away. And in the garden she forced herself upon him. He tried to resist her, but his madness overcame him. That is the explanation of the absence of a cry for help, which once I stated to be the key to the mystery. If she had been walking along that path to the house, she would have had time to cry out, no matter how quickly the assailant had sprung out at her. But she did not utter a cry because she was already in the arms of the assailant, compelling him to a passionate embrace, and without doubt it was a simple thing to strangle her silently in that very position."

"Good God!" Copplestone shuddered.

"His account of how she had asked him to find Mr. Copplestone, and tell him she was not well, and of how he had left her on her way to the house, was a succession of ingenious lies which could not be disproved. That is my story," concluded Monsieur Dupont. "The next most important point at the moment is that James Layton is cleared of a charge from which he could not possibly have saved himself."

"Layton will be released with full honors to-morrow," the inspector said.

"And I think," added Monsieur Dupont, "that there will be another matter—not unconnected with a young lady named Jenny West—upon which we shall have to congratulate him—and with very good reason."

Chapter XXXIV

Conclusion

Half-an-hour later, when the doctor's statement had been made, Copplestone and Mrs. Astley-Rolfe stood together in the flower-laden garden.

"My dear," said the new man, "I brought you here to witness my deliverance. Yesterday, when you had left me, I made up my mind to put an end to my life. To-day I am free. The cloud has rolled away. I am fit to keep my promise—if you wish it kept."

She smiled up at him through happy tears.

"If I wish it kept!" she whispered.

"By Jove!" Copplestone exclaimed, "I believe in every miracle that has ever been reported, suggested, or hinted at, from the first hour of the world!"